MW00526682

Dear Reader,

If you thought there were no more Oz books after the original fourteen by L. Frank Baum, do we have a marvelous treat in store for you. Ruth Plumly Thompson, named the new Royal Historian of Oz after Baum's death, continued the series for nineteen volumes. And we will be reviving these wonderful books, which have been out of print and unattainable anywhere for almost twenty years.

Readers who are familiar with these books swear that they are just as much fun as the originals. Thompson brought to Oz an extra spice of charming humor and an added richness of imagination. Her whimsical use of language and deftness of characterization make her books a joy to read—for adults and children alike.

If this is your first journey into Oz, let us welcome you to one of the most beloved fantasy worlds ever created. And once you cross the borders, beware—you may never want to leave.

Happy Reading,
Judy-Lynn and Lester del Rey

THE WONDERFUL OZ BOOKS
Now Published by Del Rey Books

By L. Frank Baum

#1 The Wizard of Oz
#2 The Land of Oz
#3 Ozma of Oz
#4 Dorothy and the Wizard in Oz
#5 The Road to Oz
#6 The Emerald City of Oz
#7 The Patchwork Girl of Oz
#8 Tik-Tok of Oz
#9 The Scarecrow of Oz
#10 Rinkitink in Oz
#11 The Lost Princess of Oz
#12 The Tin Woodsman of Oz
#13 The Magic of Oz
#14 Glinda of Oz

By Ruth Plumly Thompson

#15 The Royal Book of Oz
#16 Kabumpo in Oz
#17 The Cowardly Lion of Oz
#18 Grampa in Oz
#19 The Lost King in Oz
#20 The Hungry Tiger of Oz
#21 The Gnome King of Oz
#22 The Giant Horse of Oz
#23 Jack Pumpkinhead of Oz
#24 The Yellow Knight of Oz
#25 Pirates in Oz
#26 The Purple Prince of Oz
*#27 Ojo in Oz
*#28 Speedy in Oz
*#29 The Wishing Horse of Oz

*Forthcoming

Pirates in
OZ

by
Ruth Plumly Thompson
Founded on and continuing the Famous Oz Stories

by
L. Frank Baum
"Royal Historian of Oz"

with illustrations by
John R. Neill

A Del Rey Book
Ballantine Books • New York

A Del Rey Book
Published by Ballantine Books

Copyright The Reilly & Lee Co., 1931; Copyright The Reilly &
Lee Company in care of Henry Regnery Company, 1959

"The Marvelous Land of Oz" Map Copyright © 1979 by James
E. Haff and Dick Martin. Reproduced by permission of The International Wizard of Oz Club, Inc.

"The Magical Countries Surrounding Oz" Map Copyright © 1980
by James E. Haff and Dick Martin. Reproduced by permission of
The International Wizard of Oz Club, Inc.

Cover design by Georgia Morrissey
Cover illustration by Michael Herring
Text design by Gene Siegel

Library of Congress Catalog Card Number: 85-90887

ISBN: 345-33099-4

This edition published by arrangement with Contemporary Books,
Inc.

Manufactured in the United States of America

BVG 01

SHIP AHOY!

This pirate story is dedicated,
with a little nod and wink, to

George F. MacEwan,

the only real voyageur and
able-bodied seaman I know!

Ruth Plumly Thompson.

List of Chapters

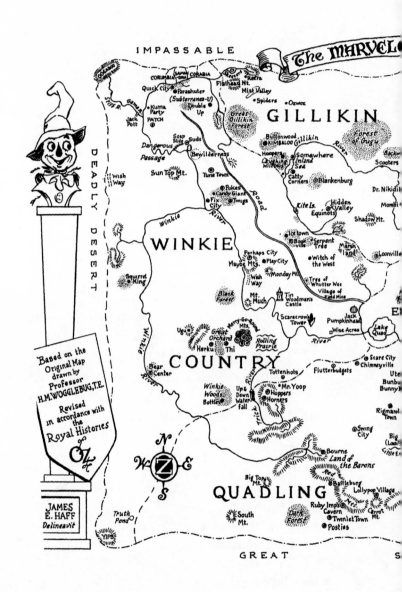

IMPASSABLE

The MARVEL

CLOUDLAND
CORUMBIA
SAMM DRAI CORABIA
Flathead Mt.
Herku
Mist Valley
Spiders
Ozwoz

Quick City
Parashuter
(Subterranea-U)
Double Up
Kusma Party
PATCH

Stiff R.
Gams
Jack Pott

Jack Pott

GILLIKIN

Great
Gillikin
Forest

Buttonwood
KIMBALOO Gillikin

Forest
of Gugu

Soap
Slide Suds
Dangerous
Passage
Bewilderness

Hoppers
Crushing
Willows
Somewhere
Inland
Sea

Backw
Scooters

Wish
Way

Sun Top Mt.

Tune Town

Catty
Corners
Blankenburg

Dr. Nikidik

DEADLY DESERT

Pokes
Candy Giant
Fix
City
Twigs

Kite Is.
Equinots
Hidden
Valley

Shadow Mt.

Mombi

WINKIE

Winkie
River

Road

Ice Town
Book
ville
Serpent
Tree
Marsh
land

Loonville

Perhaps City
Maybe Mt.
Play City
Monday Mt.
Wish
Way

Witch of
the West

Tree of
Whutter Wee
Village of
Field Mice

Squirrel
King

Mt.
Much

Tin
Woodman's
Castle

COUNTRY

Black
Forest

Merry-Go-Round
Mts.
Great
Orchard
Thi
Rolling
Prairie

Scarecrow's
Tower

Jack
Pumpkinhead
Wise Acres

E

Ugu
Herku

Lake
Quad

Bear
Center

Winkie
Woods
Bottle

Up &
Down
Water
fall

Mr. Yoop
Hoppers
Horners

Tottenhots

Flutterbudgets

Scare City
Chimneyville

Ute

Winkie
River

Trick River

Bunbu
Bunny

Rigmarol
Town

Based on the
Original Map
drawn by
Professor
H.M.WOGGLEBUG,T.E.
Revised
in accordance with
the
Royal Histories
OZ

N
W Z E
S

Swing
City
Big
(Loud
Little E

Bourne
Land of
the Barons
Red

QUADLING

Big Tom
Mt.

Baffleburg
Lollypop Village

JAMES
E. HAFF
Delineavit

Truth
Pond

YIPS

South
Mt.

Dark
Forest

Ruby Imps
Cavern
Carrot
Mt.
Twnlet Town
Postias

GREAT

S

LAND of OZ

DESERT

Agoochie Mt. Gilkenny

Gayelette's Palace

MPERDINK
Follensby Forest
Rith Metic
Illumi Nation (U)
Soup Sea
Tattypoo

River Road

Winged Monkeys

Gapers Gulch Headland

REGALIA Highlanders (Hook Noses)

Silver Mt. Turn Town
KERETARIA

COUNTRY

Magic Isle Lake O SHIFTING SANDS

Lonesome Duck

Dr. Pipt Ojo Cave City (U) Sapphire City (Ozure Isles)

Blue Forest Munchkin Mts.

Uptown Foolish Owl & Wise Donkey Round-abouties

Torpedo Town (U)
Stair Way (U)
Delves (U)

Man-eating Plants Road

Yoop Castle Nimmie Amee Swynes Mt. Munch!

Dragons (U) Tripedalia Invisible Country

MUNCHKIN Jinjur Bandits' Cave

Squee-Gee-ville Blue Forest

Shutter Town White Mts.

Kalidahs Ku-Klip

First Yellow Brick Road Where Dorothy's House landed

Fiddlestick Forest Stone Mt. Poppy Field Reach Scarecrow Beanpole (Middlings and Silver Islanders Underground)

River Rolling Road

Wogglebug College Dicksyland Easter Bunny (U) HALIDOM TROTH

Miss uttenclip Elevator Man Sign Here Preservatory

Fuddlecumjig Mooer Mt. (Bear Mt.) Link

Pineville Unicorners Tappy Town COUNTRY

Story-Blossom Mt. Good Children Crystal City Crystal Mt. Travelers' Tree

Morrow Green Mt. Snow Mt. Shamsbad

Blue Forest SEEBANIA

China Country Pine Woods Roundabout

Dick Tater Crinklink Drumbad (U)

View Halloo Gorba's Garden (U) Hah Hoh Humbad

merheads COUNTRY

op Great Waterfall Red Mt. Doorways

nda's Palace JINXLAND RAGBAD MUDGE

Y WASTE

©1980 by James E. Haff and Dick Martin

Published by The International Wizard of Oz Club by Royal Appointment of Her Gracious Majesty OZMA of OZ MCMLXXX

DICK MARTIN Sculpsit

The MAGICAL COU[NTRIES]

NONESTIC OCEAN

o Nowhere   Snow Is.   Isa Poso   Thunder Mt. / Lightning Lake

Conjo Is.   W Z E S N   Regos Coregos   Mount Up   Volcano Is.   Red Jinn's Castle   Nome

Shell City   Octagon Is.   Pingaree   Rose Kingdom   Zeron Mts.   Valley of Romance   LAND   Field of Feathers

Ruggedo's Island   Salamander Is. (Lavaland)   Impossipillio Is.   Elbow Is.   Blaze's Volcano (Fire Is.–U.)   Rubber Country   DOMINIONS (Underground)   Rusty Ore   RASH   Too Much

Patrippany Is.   Biggenlittle R.   MENANKYPOO   Bridge   Entrance to Nome King's Cavern   Giant with Hammer   OF   Immense City   Down Town (U)   Rash R.   IMPASS

Peaken-spire Is.   Roaraway Is.   Norroway Is.   Gilgad   Evna   Fairy Beavers   Flame Folk   Nome King's Tunnel (U)   GILLIK   LA

Sea Forest   Davy Jones   RINKITINK   EV   NOME KING'S   Evna   Underground River   Route of Magic Carpet   DEADLY DESERT   WINKIE   COUNTRY

Ne-leega   Jumping Off Place   Squeedonia   River   Mt. Phantastico   Mt. Illuso   QUADL

To Ozamaland   Rock Is.   WHIMSIES   RIPPLE LAND   PHANFASMS & MIMICS   GROWLEYWOGS   KINGDOM of DREAMS   GREAT

A Map of the Wondrous Lands that lie beyond the Great Desert Barriers of OZ   VEGETABLE KINGDOM of MANGABOO (U)   VALLEY OF VOE (U)   Sugar Pyramids   Pyramid Mt., (U) / Gargoyles, (U) & Dragonettes (U)   Route of Sand Boat   Scoodlers (Mifkits)   Musicker   AROL

Balloon Is.   BOBOLAND   The Crescent Moon   Jalacasco Islands   Dunkiton   Foxville   Pool of Names

NONESTIC

IES *Surrounding* OZ

Isle of Dork

Roly Rogues Is.

The Sea Fairies

NONESTIC

INGDOM
OF IX

City of Ix

Nole

North Mts

Roly-Rogues

NOLAND

OCEAN

Aquareine's Palace
(Undersea)

Isle of
Phreex

SKAMPAVIA

Valley
of Lost
Things

Valley of
Toy Animals

Valley
of
Pussy-
cats

MERRY
-LAND

Valley of
Clowns

Valley of
Bonbons

Valley
of
Dolls

Valley of
Babies

Palace of
Romance

Isle
of Mifkets

Pirate Is.

LE   DESERT

COUNTRY

SHIFTING   SANDS

D OF

MUNCHKIN

EMERALD
CITY

Z

COUNTRY

COUNTRY

Heelers

RIVER

LOLAND
HILAND

Loo Hie

Island of
Civilized Monkeys

ORKLAND

The Enchanted
Forest of Lurla

HEG

AURIEL SPOR DAWNA

Twi

PLENTA

Isle of Yew

NDY   WASTE

Groves
of Trom

Lerd

Caves of the
Daemons

st LAUGHING

VALLEY of

zee

HO HAHO

UMBIA

Bumpy
Man

Turvyland (v)

Maetta

Seventon

MACVELT

MULGRAVIA

KINGDOM
OF
SCOWLEYOW

VALLEY
OF MO

(Phunnyland)

Maple Syrup
River

Mt Mern

Jackdaws'
Nest

Fistikins

AURISSAU

RIBDIL

Martlaf

JUNKUM

QUOK

BILKON

OCEAN

To Pessim's
Island

King
Anko

Based on the
Original Map
drawn by
Professor
H.M.WOGGLEBUG,T.E.

James E. Haff
Del.
Dick Martin
sculp

©1980 by James E Haff and Dick Martin

CHAPTER 1
The Outcast Gnome

ALL morning the little gray peddler had trudged along the rocky road without encountering a single customer. In his sack he carried a supply of dark spectacles which he  traded for food, old clothes, a night's lodging or whatever he could coax from the good wives of the countryside. The sun was hot and scorching and the peddler's temper, never of the best, mounted with each step he took up the stony pathway. Finally, flinging down his pack, he stamped both feet, shook both fists, and drawing a small writing tablet from his pocket began scribbling so fast and furiously that the point flew off his pencil at the fifth word. Ripping off the sheet, he threw both it and the pencil into a pepper bush and scowled fiercely at a crow that had settled on the branch of a dead tree nearby. Paying no attention to his terrible look, the crow flew down, picked up the piece of paper and holding it in one claw began to read the scribbled words.

"Haw, haw! Caw, caw!" chortled the crow, rocking backward and forward with amusement. "I know who *you* are, old bow-legs! You're the old Gnome King and bad as you ever were. Haw, haw! You're a caution, Rug! Where did you learn all this mad language anyway? Trying to conquer Oz and outwit the Wizard?" Tucking the paper under his wing, the crow stared insolently at the ragged elf who had once been King of all the Gnomes and whose last attempt to capture the Emerald City had brought him to the sorry condition of wanderer and outcast. Ruggedo made no answer to the crow's saucy speech, not because he couldn't think of plenty of things to say, but because it was impossible for him to say them. Ruggedo was speechless and the chest that had once sparkled with precious gems and heavy gold chains now bore only a rudely printed placard: "Kindly help the dumb." But though the old gnome could no longer speak, he could still act. Seizing a jagged stone he hurled it at

2

the crow with such speed and suddenness that the latter stopped crowing in a hurry and flew screeching into the air. Left to himself, Ruggedo began to weep from pure vexation and self pity, wiping his tears on his long white whiskers and kicking his heels vindictively against the rocks.

"Every one is against me!" reflected the gnome bitterly. "Every one, every two, every three, and everybody! Even the birds crow over me and make my life miserable and all because I want to regain my own kingdom and punish that wretched Ozma of Oz for defying and enchanting me!" This was not quite true, but Ruggedo's thoughts were as crooked and twisted as his crooked little body. He could not think straight nor honestly and would not admit, even to himself, that most of his troubles were his own fault.

As ruler of the gnomes he had been one of the richest and most important of monarchs, his underground dominions were vast, grand and awe inspiring, and all the precious metals and jewels an emperor could wish for had been quarried from the mines by his patient little subjects. Besides all this, Ruggedo had had many magic treasures that enabled him to overcome his enemies and pass the time pleasantly between battles. But this foolish King had not been satisfied with his own possessions.

Across the Deadly Desert from his dominions lay the wonderful Land of Oz, ruled over by Princess Ozma, a fairy much more important

3

and powerful than himself. Again and again Ruggedo had tried to vanquish Ozma and conquer her kingdom. But good magic is always better than bad, and each time Ozma had triumphed over the Gnome King and his wicked allies. Naturally kindhearted and gentle, Ozma had not wished to destroy her enemy utterly. Once he had been dipped into the Fountain of Oblivion and forgot for a season his evil plans and schemings. But this did not last long and soon he was again storming the Emerald City, Ozma's capital. This time he lost not only his kingdom, but was banished, as well, to a lonely island in the Nonestic Ocean. Miraculously escaping from this island on an old pirate ship, Ruggedo had made a last desperate attempt to enslave the Oz folk. But this scheme, too, had

proved vain, and the silence stone flung by Peter, a Philadelphia boy visiting in Oz, just at the moment Ruggedo was consigning Ozma and all the celebrities to the bottom of the sea, had struck the Gnome King on the forehead and rendered him speechless. The spell cast by the silence stone would keep Ruggedo dumb for seven years, and thinking this punishment enough Ozma had let him go.

For five years now the former Metal Monarch had wandered up and down Oz, begging, peddling, and stealing. Finally, homesick and discouraged, he had bribed an eagle to carry him across the Deadly Desert and had thus returned to his own country in Ev. But Kaliko, appointed by Ozma to rule in his stead, would not even buy one pair of spectacles from his former master, and calling his bodyguards had had Ruggedo thrown out of his underground castle in short order. So now the dejected little gnome was on his way to the Kingdom of Rinkitink which lay just beyond Gnoman's Land bordering the Nonestic Ocean. It was ruled over by a king so cheerful and merry that Ruggedo felt he could not only sell him a lot of spectacles, but hoax the old monarch into giving him a position at court as well. The mere thought of King Rinkitink made Ruggedo stop weeping, and taking another pencil from his pocket he began sharpening it briskly. Writing messages upon his tablet was the only way Ruggedo could make himself understood and he wanted to be quite ready to converse with his jolly old neighbor.

"Why, I may even be able to steal some of his magic," reasoned Ruggedo, squinting down at the long point he had put on his pencil. Thinking of magic always put him in a good humor and picking up his sack he proceeded more hopefully along the rocky road. In about an hour he had come to a narrow crevice between two rocks and squeezing through found himself on the edge of a small and unknown country. Sure that the mountain pass would lead directly into Rinkitink, the Gnome King paused uncertainly. On the maps in his underground castle, he had often studied the kingdoms near his own dominions. To the north lay the Vegetable Kingdom, Rinkitink, and the Land of the Wheelers. Ruggedo had been travelling north and had visited all these places, but the country he was now entering was entirely new and unfamiliar to him. As far as he could see stretched a flowering garden. Its posies were old-fashioned and quiet in color: faded pinks, light blues and subdued lavenders. The trees and grass seemed more gray then green, and over the whole hung a silvery haze that gave an air of dreamy unreality to the scene. Ruggedo much preferred the flash and glitter of his jewelled caverns and looking contemptuously at the pale yellow palace rising from the center of the garden, he wondered what kind of king it might contain. The palace was surrounded by a high rose-grown wall and as Ruggedo continued to stare, a door in the wall opened and out stepped a stately courtier in a fine white wig. He had a large sign under his arm. This he hung on the golden doorknob, and after looking up and down the road, yawned tremendously and went in, shutting the door behind him.

Extremely curious as to just what the sign might say, Ruggedo jumped down from the rocky ledge and went scurrying across the garden. It was strangely quiet and still; the birds hopping about in the branches of the trees neither twittered nor sang and Ruggedo's own footsteps sounded so loud and startling that by the time he reached the castle he was uneasily proceeding on tiptoe. Quite out of breath, for he had hurried considerably, he squinted up at the notice on the door. Then he gave a bounce of pure astonishment.

```
WANTED:

A DUMB KING
```

stated the sign in calm pink letters. Ruggedo could have screamed with surprise and shock, but this being impossible, he bounded into the air and kicked both heels together, his wicked little face crimson with excitement.

"Can it be that at last I am to have some good fortune?" exulted the old gnome, his red eyes snapping with anticipation. "I am a king; for the present, I am dumb. Surely, then, this must mean *me!*" Snatching down the sign he tucked it under his arm and opening the door in the wall walked boldly into the courtyard.

CHAPTER 2

The Strange Kingdom of Menankypoo

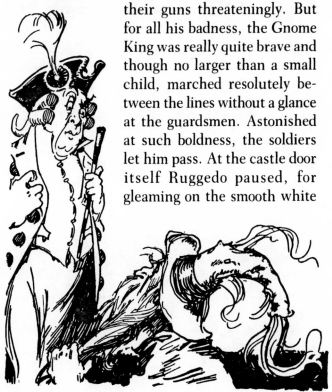

A DOUBLE line of guardsmen, in pale yellow uniforms and three cornered hats, stretched from the gates to the castle door, and as Ruggedo burst into the courtyard they raised their guns threateningly. But for all his badness, the Gnome King was really quite brave and though no larger than a small child, marched resolutely between the lines without a glance at the guardsmen. Astonished at such boldness, the soldiers let him pass. At the castle door itself Ruggedo paused, for gleaming on the smooth white panels were eight jewelled words: "This is the Kingdom of MENANKYPOO. Quiet, please."

"Suits me!" sniffed Ruggedo, and straightening the placard on his chest, he confidently kicked open the door. His entrance caused quite a commotion and stir in the yellow throne room. The courtiers and ministers of Menankypoo, who had been drowsing peacefully in the depths of the great yellow armchairs, sprang to their feet and looked askance at the ragged figure in the doorway, and Ruggedo as curiously looked back. At first glance they seemed quite usual and every day sort of fellows, but as a tall pompous dignitary with a gold staff hurried forward he realized his error. Here, surely, were the oddest people he had encountered in the whole thousand years of his existence, for the Menankypoos did not talk at all. But their foreheads, which were high and broad, lit up with long sparkling sentences, each message as clear and distinct as words flashed upon an electric sign.

"I am Kapoosa, Major Dumbo of Menankypoo," announced the fellow with the staff, tapping three times on the floor. "Who are you?" Blinking up at the Major Dumbo and almost too startled to answer, Ruggedo held up the sign he had taken from the castle gate and pointing to the words, "Dumb King," waited for Kapoosa to continue the conversation.

"So—you—are—a—dumb—king?" Rather slowly the words formed on Kapoosa's forehead and the Menankypoos, looking curiously over his shoulder, spelled out all sorts of uncomplimentary remarks and questions. To these Ruggedo paid no attention whatever, but taking out his tablet and pencil scribbled hurriedly: "What are the duties of the king?"

"The king is not supposed to do anything." This answer, which presently appeared on the Major Dumbo's forehead, exactly suited the lazy little Gnome King. So pushing imperiously through the crowd of Menankypoos he made his way to the throne, felt its cushions fastidiously and finding them soft and numerous settled down contentedly and wrote: "I'll take the job." The Menankypoos looked doubtfully at one another as they read the words on Ruggedo's tablet, and started such an agitated conversation among themselves that the room became fairly electric from the flashes. While they were thus engaged, Ruggedo suddenly thought of something else.

"What became of your last king?" he scrawled uneasily.

"He fell in the sea. As it is customary for the King of Menankypoo to do nothing he continued to do nothing, and consequently sank to the bottom. That is all." Ruggedo thoughtfully considered the fate of Menankypoo's monarch as it was spelled out on Kapoosa's forehead. At first he was tempted to inquire why they had not fished the king out of the sea, for in fairy countries sovereigns are not destroyed or killed by such simple accidents. But realizing that this would deprive him of the kingship, he merely

pursed up his lips and nodded understandingly. The Menankypoos had by this time come to some agreement and after a short conference with them Kapoosa stepped closer to the throne.

"You must now pass the dumb tests," read Ruggedo, after a long, earnest stare into the grave face of the Major Dumbo, and without enlightening him any further the Menenkypoos filed out of the throne room.

"Now what?" thought the puzzled gnome. "I cannot talk and am therefore dumb, but there may be more to it than that. It will be hard for a fellow as smart as I am to pass for a dunce. Still, I must manage it somehow." Pushing back his straggling locks, Ruggedo pressed his hands to his temples, closed his little red eyes and thought and thought and presently reached a very clever conclusion. "As I am naturally bright

12

and sharp, to pass this test I must do the exact opposite to what I would naturally do," he decided, reasonably enough. Feeling that he had already solved the problem, Ruggedo sank back among his cushions and waited for what was to come. He was not long in suspense for almost at once a kitchen boy in heavy wooden shoes darted through a door. Before Ruggedo had time to think he jumped hard on the Gnome King's favorite foot.

"Brine and brimstone!" raged Ruggedo, but alas! only to himself, for he could not utter one sound. Hopping on the other foot he made a savage swing at the kitchen boy, but the boy was already half way to the kitchen. The Menankypoos, peering through curtains and doors, nodded their heads with satisfaction and approval. Noting this out of the corner of his eye Ruggedo grew calmer. Recalling that kingdoms are not gained without some trouble and discomfort he sat down, his injured foot stuck straight out before him. Scarcely had he recovered from the shock of the first test before the great central doors of the throne room banged open and in stepped the Yellow Guardsmen. They stamped forward stolidly, six abreast, and Ruggedo, clutching the arms of his throne, tried to make up his mind what to do or what not to do. The sensible thing would be, of course, to write "HALT!" on his tablet and hold it up before they advanced any further. But one did not pass dumb tests by acting sensibly, so shutting his eyes and gritting his crooked teeth Ruggedo did nothing.

Thump! Thump! Thump! On came the Yellow Guardsmen; they reached the throne and without pause or stop tramped right over the little Gnome King and on out through a door at the back. There were a good many guardsmen and by the time they had all passed, Ruggedo was perfectly flat on his back. Only the number and softness of the cushions saved him from being completely squashed. Rather slowly Ruggedo straightened up, feeling his nose to see if it was still in place, rubbing his stomach, and turning his neck stiffly and experiementally from left to right. As he was trying to bend his knees the tap of the Major Dumbo's staff made him look up. Before the throne stood six regal ladies, gowned with extreme elegance, but all exactly alike.

"Your Highness will now pick out the Royal Princess," flashed Kapoosa in one bright sentence. By this time Ruggedo was so mad he could hardly breathe and the eyes he turned on the six royal maidens snapped so red and spitefully that they all took a step backward. But ruffled and enraged as he was, Ruggedo still wanted to be king. Long experience had taught the gnome that princesses were usually plainer than their ladies-in-waiting. So, after a careful squint all down the line, he pointed to the loveliest of the Menankypoo maidens. This one he felt sure could not be the real princess. His choice seemed to delight the Major Dumbo, who jumped lightly into the air and clicked both heels together. Leaning forward to see what he was saying, Ruggedo read with some satisfaction:

"This person has passed the dumb tests. He cannot talk, he cannot act, he cannot think. He will make a splendid king! Long live the King of Menankypoo!" As this sentence lit up the forehead of the Major Dumbo, all the other courtiers hurried into the court room bowing and smiling. "Long live the King," flashed from face to face.

"I won't live long if I have to pass many more days like this," thought Ruggedo gloomily, but pulling himself together he bowed first to the left, then to the right and nodded haughtily, or as haughtily as a fellow who has just been trampled upon can nod, to his future subjects. Kapoosa was the first to reach the throne. Handing the king a pair of golden dumb-bells he explained in a series of flashes that if Ruggedo wanted anything he had merely to raise one or the other of the dumb-bells and a page would at once appear to carry out his commands. The Menankypoos, he went on to say, did not desire an ambitious monarch who was always making wars and conquests. They preferred him to mind his own business and to allow them to meditate and converse in quietness and peace. All this took some time, and when the Major Dumbo had finished, Ruggedo, who was quite worn out with so much sight reading, seized his tablet and scrawled imperiously. "Go! I wish to be alone."

With little nods and shrugs the Menankypoos withdrew and as the last yellow robe swished through the doorway Ruggedo raised one of the golden dumb-bells. To the yellow page who sprang up apparently from nowhere he handed a slip of paper on which he had written. "Bring four breakfasts and a bottle of liniment, at *once!*" The breakfasts were brought and served by a very dumb waiter, the liniment by the page. Breakfast was Ruggedo's favorite repast and after he had finished all four and directed the page to rub the back of his neck with the liniment he heaped a pile of pillows under his head and stretched out luxuriously on his new throne.

"I dare say it's going to be dreadfully dull and dumb here," meditated the Gnome King, drow-

sily waving his attendants away, "but at any rate
I shall have a good rest. Hah, hoh, *hum!*" After
his long years of banishment and the weary miles
of tramping, the throne of Menankypoo felt so
soft and delicious that Ruggedo fell asleep and
never waked at all for three and a half days. At
the end of the third day, he arose and began to
take a little interest in his kingdom. The royal
robes of the former monarch were taken in to
fit his funny, crooked little figure, and decked
out in shiny satin coat and knee breeches, and
wearing a crown at least a foot high, he strutted
proudly about the castle and up and down the
streets of the silent city. But even so, Ruggedo
was very far from happy.

It was bad enough not to be able to talk himself, but never to hear anyone else talk was
dreadful indeed. The very animals in Menan-

kypoo were dumb animals and the gnome, used to the talking beasts of Ev and Oz, kicked the castle cat from sheer disappointment when he found that it could say nothing, not even "Mew!" The Menankypoos sat about the pleasant gardens holding endless conversations in their strange sign language or gazing dreamily into space. They were easy-going and pleasant enough fellows, but their life seemed fearfully dull to the restless little Gnome King.

At first it amused him to wander about the capital at night and see the streets illuminated by the bright conversation and light talk of his subjects but he soon tired of this, and often in the throne room, when his ministers and advisers assembled for a conference, the flash and glow from their foreheads was so annoying that Ruggedo was forced to wear his dark spectacles. Seeing what people say and hearing what they say are entirely different matters and the monarch of Menankypoo longed for the sound of a friendly voice. Even an unfriendly one would have been welcome. There were no magic appliances in the castle and after he had examined all the jewels and counted all the gold pieces in the treasury, tried on each of his regal robes and reviewed the Yellow Guardsmen a dozen times at least, Ruggedo sank down on his throne and yawning terrifically wondered what to do next. With all the riches and resources of Menankypoo at his disposal it seemed a shame to sit still and do nothing.

The Strange Kingdom of Menankypoo

"Do you realize that with an army like ours, we could conquer every kingdom around here?" he wrote on his tablet one morning when he and Taka, the fat chancellor of Menankypoo, were breakfasting in the garden.

"How would Your Majesty like to take a little walk along the sea wall?" The Gnome King, spelling out this question on the fat forehead of his chancellor, saw Taka wink at Kapoosa and make a slight pushing gesture.

"Hah, if I grow troublesome, they mean to shove me into the sea, as they probably shoved their former ruler," thought the crafty gnome, and shaking his head in a vigorous "No" at Taka, he said no more of conquering. After all, it was better to be a dumb king in Menankypoo than a dumb and despised peddler in Oz. But every day the silence in the yellow castle grew more oppressive, and Ruggedo spent much of his time wandering along the sea shore by himself, thinking of old times and battles. One morning, after an unusually long walk, he dropped down on a boulder to rest. The coast at this point was particularly rough and rugged and back of him rose a sheer wall of irregular rocks. Looking idly at the jagged mass, Ruggedo noticed a yellow cross on one of the stones. Tucking up his satin cloak, he scrambled upward and discovered that the rock thus marked was really a door. Extremely interested and excited, Ruggedo pressed his shoulder against the rock and pushed with all his might. But all his might was not very mighty and the door refused to budge. Then, suddenly remembering his magic, Ruggedo pushed the rock right on the yellow cross. Instantly and noiselessly it swung inward and Ruggedo, not expecting it to open so quickly, plunged headlong into a dim, damp cavern. A yellow lantern suspended by a chain from the ceiling cast a weird and wavering light over the rocky interior and under the lantern hung a crooked yellow sign:

THIS IS THE CAVE OF
KADJ THE CONJURER.

Ruggedo, from his exceedingly uncomfortable position on the floor, had just succeeded in reading the sign when the door, with a whirr and a bang that blew out the lantern, slammed shut, leaving him in utter darkness.

CHAPTER 3
A Bright Idea Strikes the King

NOW gnomes, like cats and owls, can see in the dark, and Ruggedo's red eyes flashed fearsomely around the conjurer's cave. His first glance told him that Kadj was not at  home. Panting with relief, for it is extremely dangerous to burst unawares upon strange magicians, Ruggedo rose and began tiptoeing cautiously about. The stone floor was covered with heavy rugs, the walls hung with jewelled swords and daggers, mystic maps and magic charts, while in every corner and available space stood monstrous metal chests studded with gems. There were no chairs nor tables but strewn about were quantities of soft cushions, and a bubbling green pool in the center filled the air with strange, uneasy murmurs. As the Gnome King reached the farthest end of the rocky room, a fire sprang up in the grate, and burning without wood or coal sent its long, flickering blue and yellow lights into every corner of the cavern.

"If I can just steal some magic and get off before this fellow returns everything will be fine," decided Ruggedo, with a greedy glance at the conjurer's chests. Rushing over to the nearest one he tried to lift the lid. But the chest was locked by some magic and secret process. So were they all, and after trying each one in turn the gnome, in furious disappointment, jumped five times into the air and kicked a red cushion into the fireplace. But this did not help matters and only filled the cave with smoke. So, quieting down, Ruggedo began to examine the walls for secret cupboards or shelves and soon he discovered a small door under a bright piece of tapestry.

SURE CURE FOR EVERYTHING

said a notice on the door. Without a moment's hesitation Ruggedo turned the knob.

"There may be something in here to restore my speech," thought the excited little fellow, tugging frantically at the knob. Unlike the chests,

A Bright Idea Strikes the King

it opened quite easily and down fell a blunt axe, striking Ruggedo such a blow on the forehead that he sailed through the air and fell with a terrific plunk into the green pond. Three times he sank under the bubbling waves, but the third time up he managed to grasp the rocky edge of the pool and pull himself out.

"Blazes and bluing!" blubbered the monarch of Menankypoo through his chattering teeth. "Willy goats and wildcats! If I had that conjurer I'd wring his neck—I'd—" His voice grew louder and louder, higher and higher, and finally died away in a frightened squeak. "Why, I'm shouting out loud!" sputtered the startled gnome, his eyes bulging with astonishment. "I can talk! I can sing! I can hear myself think!"

Flinging away his pencil Ruggedo began to laugh, cheer and yell at the top of his new found

23

voice. There was a large lump on his forehead
from the axe, and he was still wet and shivering
from his plunge in the pool, but scarcely noticing
these discomforts the delighted old elf ran shouting around the cave till his breath and his legs
gave out together and he sank down exhausted
on a heap of cushions. There he became calmer.
Reflecting that any more noise might bring the
owner of the cave he stopped shouting, but he
could not refrain from whispering happily to
himself just to see whether the enchantment of
the silence stone had really been dispelled by
the blow of the axe and the waters of the green
pool. His voice, not heard for five long years,
seemed perfectly beautiful to him and we cannot
blame the little rascal for holding long and flow-
ery conversations with himself.

Finally, fully convinced of his cure, Ruggedo
hurried to the door of the cave. Clever as Kadj
had proved himself to be, the Gnome King did
not wish to run the risk of any more enchant-
ments and was anxious to leave before the conjurer's return. He had not decided upon any
plan, but having regained his speech he felt that
it was but a question of time before he would
regain his old kingdom and revenge himself upon
Ozma and her councillors. But entering the conjurer's cave was one thing, leaving it quite another; and though Ruggedo pushed, pulled and
pounded, though he tried long incantations and
mysterious passes, the rock door refused to open.
Horrors! What good was it to have his speech

restored if he was to be sealed up in a hidden
cavern at the mercy of a strange and powerful
sorcerer? In a panic the Gnome King raced round
and round the rocky prison, banging into the
great chests, kicking the conjurer's cushions right
and left and hammering frantically on the stony
walls. He had circled the cave twice in his search
for a hidden door or crevice and was leaning
wearily against the painted panel beside the fireplace, when he heard a sharp and mysterious
ticking. He put his ear inquiringly to the panel
and as the ticking grew louder gave the panel a
good hard push. Immediately and noiselessly it
moved aside, revealing a huge and singular looking person in yellow. Thinking it was Kadj himself, Ruggedo jumped back as far as he could
and with chattering knees stood looking up at
the great fellow. He was dressed in the stately
manner of the Menankypoos, but his head was
of wood and his face was the face of a clock. As
Ruggedo continued to gaze up at him the Clock
Man, with a broad wink, stepped out of the
narrow aperture and walking over to the mirror
above the fireplace regarded himself long and
critically. By this time Ruggedo's curiosity had
got the better of his fright and pattering after
the Clock Man he tugged excitedly at his cloak.

"I see by your dress and bearing that you are
a subject of Menankypoo. I, for the present, am
its king, and as we are both caught in this miserable cave let us put our heads together and
see what can be done." The Clock Man, who

was polishing his glass face with a silk handkerchief, turned round at Ruggedo's question
and studied the gnome closely and curiously.
Then he sat down upon a near-by chest, put his
finger tips together and closed his eyes. It was
exactly five minutes before twelve by his clock
face, and Ruggedo, expecting him to speak in
the same sign language as his other subjects,
waited anxiously for his forehead to light up.
But nothing of the kind happened and four minutes ticked off in silence. Only the great size of
the fellow kept Ruggedo from jumping on his
foot or kicking him violently in the shins. Pacing
impatiently up and down, the tempery little gnome
finally sprang up on a chest opposite.

"Are you deaf?" he screeched angrily. "Are
you dumb? Can't you even make signs?"

At Ruggedo's rude cries the Clock Man stood
up and a little door in his forehead flew open.
A yellow bird perched in the doorway gave twelve
shrill cuckoos and then with a whirr and a bang
whizzed straight at the Gnome King, striking
him with such force and suddenness that he fell
over like a toy soldier shot with a cork gun.
Bounding up in a fury, Ruggedo was just in time
to see the yellow bird dart back to its little com-
partment, the door shut, and the Clock Man
stifle a well-bred yawn. Not only was he a Clock
Man, mind you, but a Cuckoo Clock Man!
Snatching off his crown, Ruggedo was on the
point of hurling it at the creature's head, when
a slip of yellow paper the bird had left on the

26

A YELLOW BIRD WHIZZED AT THE GNOME KING

chest attracted his attention. Muttering and sputtering, Ruggedo picked up the paper and read what was written there.

"I am Clocker, the Wise Man of Menankypoo, banished to the conjurer's cave for putting bright ideas into the head of the former king. As my rescuer, I thank you, and will give you the same good counsel I gave to my former master. My first advice is: 'Hold your tongue!' How does this strike Your Majesty?"

For a moment Ruggedo stared at the paper, too dumbfounded for words. Then, throwing caution to the winds, he rushed at the Cuckoo Clock Man and began to thump and hammer him with both fists.

"How dare you address me in this outrageous fashion, you old false alarm, you? I'll have you baked, boiled and beheaded for this!" shouted the enraged little gnome.

Clocker did not seem greatly alarmed by these dreadful threats, and grasping Ruggedo by the collar held him out at arm's length. Then, giving him a couple of good shakes, he dropped him hard on the floor and taking a book out of his pocket sat down on the chest and calmly began to read. Considerably subdued and blinking from the shock of his fall, Ruggedo sat thoughtfully on the floor and for several moments there was not a sound in the cave except the whirr and tick of the Wise Man's works. "After all," reflected Ruggedo at last, "nothing is to be gained by quarrelling, especially with a fellow three

A Bright Idea Strikes the King

times my size." So, rising stiffly, he put on his crown and swallowing his anger began to address the Wise Man in long wheedling sentences.

"As we are both prisoners in this wretched cavern, let us be friends and try to find some way to escape together," began the Gnome King in a low voice.

The Cuckoo Clock Man looked inquiringly over his book and then nodded so pleasantly that Ruggedo went on to tell him the whole history of his life, how he had lost his own kingdom and had been banished and enchanted, how he had come to be monarch of Menankypoo, entered the conjurer's cave and miraculously regained his speech. Now, concluded the Gnome King, he was not only anxious to regain his own kingdom but to gain, as well, ascendency over the whole Land of Oz and revenge himself upon Ozma and everyone in the Emerald City. The first thing, naturally, was to escape from the cave. How, queried the wizened little elf, were they to do that? Remembering the shock of Clocker's last retort, Ruggedo sprang behind a chest and peered anxiously around the corner at the Wise Man.

Ruggedo's story had taken some time to tell and it was now a quarter past twelve, so, almost as soon as the gnome put his question, the Clock Man spoke, or rather struck again. This time the cuckoo screamed only once and quite politely carried the yellow paper down to the Gnome King. As Ruggedo read Clocker's second message, his face grew red with annoyance, but as

he was absolutely dependent upon the Wise Man for help, he managed with an effort to control himself.

A Bright Idea Strikes the King

"Keep your temper and I will help you," said the yellow slip, "and tell you more than the time. Unlike most wise men who talk continuously and say nothing, I speak every fifteen minutes. First, pick up your writing pad and pencil and, above everything, hold your tongue. If the Menankypoos discover that you can speak they will throw you into the sea. If we leave the cave together they will throw us both into the sea. Therefore you must leave the cave alone and act exactly as you did before you came here. When you reach the castle, collect as much of the gold and as many of the jewels as we can carry and hide them in a safe place. I will stay here and think up some way for us to leave Menankypoo and reach Oz. Kadj is away visiting his daughter, Cinderbutton, the witch, and will not return for a month, and as I do not require food I will be quite comfortable in the cave. On a hook by the fireplace you will find the conjurer's es-cape. Put on the cape, jump into the fire and you will instantly find yourself outside. Return to-morrow and I will have something interesting to tell you. But remember, speak one word, and all will be lost!"

Sitting on the floor Ruggedo read the message over twice. "A fire escape!" he shuddered uneasily. "Perhaps this is a trick of the Clock Man to get rid of me. Perhaps I shall be burned to a crisp!" But on the whole the Wise Man's advice seemed sensible, and finally deciding to take a

chance Ruggedo came out from behind the chest,
nodding to Clocker to show that he understood
and bagan to look around for his tablet and pencil. When he had found them he shook hands
with the Wise Man and stepped over to the
fireplace. There, sure enough, was a long red
cape hanging from a hook beside the mantel.
Wrapping himself in its voluminous folds and
feeling exceedingly frightened, Ruggedo jumbed
boldly into the fire. The last thing he saw in
the Conjurer's Cave was the Wise Man of Menankypoo looking at him warningly, his fingers to
his lips.

Then, lightly as a balloon and without the
slightest discomfort or inconvenience the Gnome
King floated up through the flames and in less
than a second found himself on the rocks outside. The cape itself had vanished and with a
gasp of relief Ruggedo realized that he was safe
and also free again. Noting carefully the location
of the cavern so that he could return again and
resolved under no curcumstance to utter a sound,
he started on a run for his castle. Halfway there,
happening to glance casually out to sea, he forgot
all his good intentions.

"Rubyation!" yelled the gnome, clapping his
hands to his head. "What does this mean?"

A great ship with red sails was bearing swiftly
down upon Menankypoo and even at that distance Ruggedo could see that her decks swarmed
with armed men.

A Bright Idea Strikes the King

"Pirates!" quavered the Gnome King, jumping behind a rock. "P-pirates!" And for once in his wicked and wrong little life, Ruggedo was right.

CHAPTER 4
The Fall of Menankypoo

R UGGEDO'S first thought should have been for his subjects but as usual Ruggedo was thinking of himself. Instead of hurrying off to warn the easy-going citizens of Menankypoo of this awful and impending peril, the gnome cowered behind the rocks and watched the pirates land. This they did in quiet and orderly fashion in the ship's small boats, until sixty of the villainous barelegged rascals had lined up on the beach. Then, grim and silent, they moved toward the city, their scimitars flashing wickedly in

the afternoon sunshine. It was almost dark when
the pirates reappeared and the Gnome King, stiff
and numb from his long wait behind the rocks,
saw that they were driving the whole population
of Menankypoo before them. Guardsmen, courtiers, men, women and children, even the little
Menankypoodles, scampered in wild confusion
before the invaders out to the very end of the
sea wall.

"Sixty against six hundred," marveled Ruggedo, shaking his head. "What fighters these
fellows must be. Brine and brimstone! There
goes Kapoosa!" And there, indeed, went the Major Dumbo, down with a mighty splash into the
sea, where he sank with well-bred resignation
and dignity to the bottom. With more interest
than sympathy the bad little gnome watched the
pirates pushing his former subjects into the water.
"Serves them right for being so dumb," muttered
Ruggedo ill-naturedly, as the last of the Yellow
Guardsmen sank beneath the waves. "A good
soaking will be good for the lazy creatures."

Now, whether or not Ruggedo was right in
his conjectures I cannot say, but the water would
certainly do them no harm, for as I said awhile
back, it is impossible to hurt or destroy beings
as magically constructed as the Menankypoos.
Not knowing how to swim or rise to the surface,
however, they clustered dumbly together at the
bottom of the sea among the fishes, discussing
anxiously the sudden and disastrous calamity
that had overtaken them. Soon the waves for

miles around were lighted with the electric flashes from their conversation. For a time the pirates amused themselves watching the lights play like phosphorescence on top of the water; then with blood-curdling yells and screeches they jumped down from the sea wall and soon the silent City of Menankypoo rang with the shouts, cheers and revelry of its conquerors. Now, Ruggedo had no desire to share the fate of his subjects and while a gnome cannot be destroyed by water, he did not intend to spend his time at the bottom of the Nonestic Ocean.

"I've suffered enough," shuddered the Gnome King, coming cautiously out from his hiding place and staring regretfully back at the comfortable castle of Menankypoo. Afraid to show himself or venture near the city, Ruggedo gloomily considered the prospect of a night on the rocks. Then, suddenly bethinking himself of Clocker and the conjurer's cave, he slid like a small gray shadow along the seashore. The moon had come up bright and full, and by its white, silvery rays, Ruggedo easily found the yellow cross that marked the entrance to the cave. The Wise Man was sitting by the fire reading and looked up in mild surprise as Ruggedo burst impetuously upon him.

"Pirates!" panted the Gnome King, waving his arms wildly, and in short, breathless sentences told all that had happened since he left the cavern. The Wise Man listened with close attention and when Ruggedo described the way the pirates had pushed the Menankypoos into the sea, he

36

positively beamed with pleasure, for he had only wheels and washers where most of us wear our hearts. Perhaps, too, he felt slightly resentful at his long imprisonment in the conjurer's cave. At any rate he seemed to find the whole story intensely amusing and his face behind its glass covering twinkled and twitched with enjoyment.

"The pirates will take all the gold and treasure and leave nothing for us at all. What are we to do now?" groaned the gnome, throwing himself down on a heap of cushions opposite Clocker. It was ten minutes past ten so he had to wait five long minutes before Clocker spoke. But the answer when it came was astonishing enough and well worth waiting for.

"We must arouse the interest and ambition of the buccaneers, and with them to help us, conquer this Land of Oz about which you have

told me," directed the paper the cuckoo dropped
into Ruggedo's lap. "When we have conquered
Oz and your former kingdom, we will destroy
the pirates and rule over all these countries ourselves."

"But how?" gasped the Gnome King, looking
up into the shining face of the Wise Man of
Menankypoo. "If we so much as show our noses
these pirates will shove us into the sea." Wrig-
gling with impatience he waited another quarter-
hour for Clocker to explain. The Cuckoo Clock
Man seemed to share Ruggedo's restlessness and
paced nervously up and down the cavern until
it was time for him to strike.

"We must coax, wheedle and flatter them,"
counselled Clocker, when at last the cuckoo
struck ten thirty. "We must promise to lead
them to new and rich countries; pretend we are
wizards, and come—we must go now, while they
are in a good humor from their victory. Come,
and you may depend on me!" The Gnome King
looked somewhat doubtful as he read the Wise
Man's advice, but Clocker, without waiting for
his consent, snatched Ruggedo by the arm and
wrapping the conjurer's cloak around them both,
jumped into the fireplace. Before the Wise Man
had ticked twice they were outside and striding
along the beach toward the castle. The more
Ruggedo considered Clocker's plan the wiser it
seemed to him and by the time they reached the
city his usual arrogance and assurance had returned. Hurrying through the castle doors which

had carelessly been left open they tramped boldly into the dining hall. The pirates were sitting around the table shouting out a lusty sea song. Stopping in the middle of a line they stared in stupefaction at the two figures in the doorway, for they were convinced that every living soul in the city had been tossed into the ocean.

"Hail, brave conquerors of Menankypoo!" began Ruggedo, springing nimbly upon a chair and taking advantage of their short, shocked silence. "I, Ruggedo the Rough, former King of the Gnomes, and Clocker, my wise man and wizard, have come to help you to further conquests and victories. *Attend*, for I would speak with the chief and captain of this band!" So proudly and imperiously had the Gnome King spoken that the pirates were impressed in spite of themselves. There were a few mutters and calls of "Toss them in the sea, mates," but no one made a move to do it.

"Let's hear what they have to say," roared a black-bearded buccaneer, thumping on the table with his dagger.

"Aye! Aye! Let them speak," rasped a red-headed rascal, jumping to his feet. "We've left our former chief for a soft-hearted lubber," explained the red-head, addressing himself to the Gnome King. "I am Peggo the Red; there sits Binx the Bad, and one or the other of us will be chief before morning." Peggo paused, and such a look of jealousy and hatred passed between the two sea robbers that Ruggedo gave a bounce of alarm. At the same time a perfectly splendid idea popped into his wicked little head.

"Let me be your chief while ashore," proposed the Gnome King. "I know this country and all about land battles. The kingdoms around here are small and poor and not worthy of such valiant fighters. Follow me and I will lead you to the marvelous Kingdom of Oz where there are more princesses, more jewels and magic treasures then you have seen in all your voyaging." Binx and Peggo exchanged a quick, greedy glance and then stared suspiciously at the ugly old gnome. While they were trying to make up their minds the Wise Man of Menankypoo struck eleven. The sudden opening of the little door in Clocker's forehead and the piercing screeches of the cuckoo threw the company into wildest confusion and when the wooden bird darted straight at Peggo

and placed a slip of paper in his hands the buccaneers cringed and grew pale beneath their
whiskers.

"Do as the Gnome King suggests," read Peggo,
the paper trembling like a leaf in his shaking
fingers. "Ruggedo is both bold and relentless.
With his help and my counsel you can conquer
the mighty Kingdom of Oz and become rich and
powerful as emperors!"

"We–e–ll, s–shall we do it?" stammered Peggo,
looking uncertainly down at Binx.

"Yes!" roared Binx, the first of the pirates to
recover his composure, and who was now thoroughly convinced that the Wise Man was a wizard. "Let's do it!" and jumping up he whispered
long and earnestly in Peggo's red ear.

"I have heard of Oz," wheezed Binx excitedly.
"It is indeed as rich and wonderful as he says.
Well, then, let these two help us with their
magic until we have conquered Oz. Then we
can do away with them and keep everything for
ourselves." Peggo nodded grimly. This would
settle the matter of their long rivalry, too. If
neither he nor Binx was chief, there would be
no need for a quarrel. "After we have conquered
Oz will be time enough for that," reflected Peggo.
Once the conquest of Oz was accomplished the
greedy pirate meant not only to destroy Binx but
the rest of the band as well. But naturally he
said nothing of this to his comrades.

"All in favor of the Gnome King for chief cry
aye!" yelled Peggo, banging on the table.

"Aye! Aye!" shouted all the pirates, their eyes popping out at the prospect of so much riches, and drawing Ruggedo and Clocker into their midst, they clamored to hear more about the wonderful Kingdom of Oz. So, taking out his tablet and pencil, the Gnome King drew them a rough map of that odd, oblong and enchanting country ruled over by the little princess and fairy, Ozma of Oz. With two lines Ruggedo divided the oblong into triangles and in each triangle printed the name of the country it represented. The north land, he told them, was the purple kingdom of the Gillikins, the eastern triangle the powerful yellow empire of the Winkies, the red southlands of Oz belonged to the

Quadlings, while to the west lay the blue country of the Munchkins. In the exact center of the map, where all the triangles met, Ruggedo

drew a circle to show the location of the capital
and the gnome explained how Ozma ruled from
the Emerald City over all four countries of Oz.

The very sound of the Emerald City made the
pirates prick up their ears, and Clocker had
struck five times before they had had enough of
it. Warming to his subject, the Monarch of
Menankypoo described in glowing sentences the
fairy capital with its emerald-encrusted streets,
buildings and palaces. He told them about the
famous Scarecrow of Oz, a live man of straw
whose magic brains and surprising cleverness
had raised him to one of the highest positions
at Ozma's court, and about the Tin Woodman,
Emperor of the Winkies, who spent most of his
time in the Emerald City. The axe of Nick
Chopper had been enchanted and one at a time
he had severed his arms, legs and finally his
head. But after each accident, Nick had had
himself repaired by a tinsmith and had finally
become a tin woodman so bright and unusual
that Ozma had made him an emperor. There
was Tik Tok, too, a copper machine man, who,
when wound up, could talk, walk and even think.
Ruggedo told them about the Patchwork Girl, a
mischievous maiden magically constructed and
brought to life, who could make funnier verses
than any of the poets in Oz. The Cowardly Lion,
the Hungry Tiger and the Iffin were not forgotten, nor the three little mortal girls, Dorothy,
Bettsy and Trot, who had come to live with
Ozma in the Royal Palace. The gnome grew

especially bitter as he told them about Dorothy, for Dorothy was the girl who had taken his belt in the first place and caused him more trouble than all the rest of Ozma's councillors put together.

"But what of the army?" asked Binx. "Has this Ozma of Oz a large, well-trained force of fighting men?" Ruggedo had to laugh at the thought of Ozma's army, for as most of us well know it consists of one tremendously tall soldier with green whiskers, a soldier so timid he has never been known to fire off his gun. The pirates roared over the grand army of Oz but grew more thoughtful when Ruggedo told about the Wizard and his many magical devices.

"Not only has Ozma my magic belt, with which she can transform anybody into any shape she wishes and transport him anywhere, but she has a wonderful fan that can blow away an army, a magic picture that tells her everything she wishes to know and so many wishing pills and thinking powders that almost nothing is too difficult for her to accomplish."

"Then what's the use of *us* trying to conquer her?" worried Peggo. "We'll only get ourselves enchanted or destroyed."

"Ah—but—" Ruggedo waved mysteriously at the Wise Man of Menankypoo. "You forget that we are also wizards. My idea is to steal Ozma's magic and then seize the capital. It would be useless to capture each country of Oz separately, for once we are in possession of the Emerald City the whole kingdom will be ours."

"But I've heard that Oz is surrounded by a Deadly Desert and that one step on its sands destroys one forever," went on Peggo. "How are we to cross that?"

"You are right," answered Ruggedo, "but Clocker will find a way for us to cross the Deadly Desert, won't you, old shiny face?" The Wise Man looked surprised and a trifle uneasy but as it was not time for him to strike, said nothing. Taking the map, Ruggedo added the strip of Deadly Desert surrounding Oz and further explained that to reach the desert they must cross the Land of the Wheelers and his own old dominions in Ev.

"Well," yawned Binx, scratching his head thoughtfully with his scimitar, "I for one should like to see Oz, and a live man stuffed with straw. I'll have him for my slave and he shall polish my boots and daggers."

"I'll take the Tin Woodman," whistled Peggo, "and those girls shall come back with us and do all the cooking and scrubbing on the *Sea Lion*, but if we are to do all this conquering we'd better get some sleep."

"Aye! Aye!" agreed the pirates heartily, and nodding, grunting and whispering among themselves, they tramped up the stair. Throwing themselves fully clothed and booted upon the lace and silken covered beds they snored so loudly

that the very rafters rattled. Ruggedo himself got little rest, for Clocker, who insisted on sharing his room, struck every quarter-hour and the yellow bird kept tapping at his head. Indeed, by morning, Ruggedo, waking from an uneasy slumber, found himself nearly buried under a mass of yellow papers the cuckoo had dropped on him during the night.

CHAPTER 5

The King of the Octagon Isle

DRUMMING his fingers idly on the arms of his Octagon throne, King Ato the Eighth sat with closed eyes listening to the sonorous voice of the Royal Reader. Having a Royal Reader saved His Majesty much annoyance, such as wearing specs, turning the pages of books, and losing his place in the morning paper. No wonder he was fonder of Roger than of anyone else in his household— I mean castlehold. No wonder Roger had a ruby perch with gold trimmings and a diamond cup for his morning orange juice. And Roger, you may be surprised to know, was a Read Bird, clever enough to pronounce all the words in the King's eight hundred volumes and wise enough to skip all the uninteresting descriptions. Holding a fat book in one claw and balancing skillfully on the other leg, he would drone on for hours, and as Ato loved

nothing so well as a lively story or take of adventure, he took Roger wherever he went and the two were well-nigh inseparable. In appearance Roger was rather unusual, about the size and coloring of a large parrot but with a kindly face of a duck and with a duck's bill. His enormous fan tail that could open and shut was like no other bird's I could ever mention, spreading high above his head, and exceedingly useful to His Majesty in sultry weather. Add to this a pleasant and jolly disposition and you can well understand King Ato's affection for his Royal Reader.

As you may never have visited Octagon Island or come across it in any of your geographies, I will tell you at once that it is eight miles east of the Isle of Pingaree, its eight sandy shores washed by the boisterous waves of the Nonestic Ocean. In the exact center of the island rises the eight-sided castle of King Ato and at suitable distances the eighty dwellings of the Octagon Islanders. The King's subjects numbered one hundred and eighty, there being forty women, sixty children and eighty men. Of the men, eight were courtiers, eight were councillors, eight were servitors, eight were farmers, eight were shop-keepers, eight were fishermen, eight were sailors, eight were soldiers, eight were scholars and artists, and eight were musicians, so that the affairs of the island were nicely balanced and everyone ate well and often. Except for their octagon-shaped faces and hats, the eight octagon buttons on their coats and the eight pockets in their suits, the Octagon Islanders were quite like us, and life on the island was pleasant and uneventful. They had everything to make them happy and contented and good King Ato had no reason for supposing them otherwise—that is, until the bright particular morning of which I am telling you. Drowsily listening to the voice of the Read Bird, Ato became suddenly aware of a great commotion in the courtyard. Next an

ear splitting bang on the octagon drum made
him sit up with a bounce. Then in through the
octagon doors burst the eight musicians in their
best uniforms followed by the eight soldiers, the
eight sailors, the eight farmers, the eight fishermen, the eight shopkeepers, the eight scholars
and artists, the eight servitors, the eight councillors and the eight courtiers.

"Ah!" sighed the King, smiling with relief.
"It's you, is it? Good morning, my dear fellows!"
But his subjects were not to be put off with good
mornings. The Octagonese trumpeter blew eight
fierce blasts upon his horn, the eight fishermen
banged their fishing rods on the floor, the eight
soldiers and sailors pointed their guns, the eight
servitors threw down their mops and aprons, the
eight scholars and artists their books and brushes,
and the eight councillors and courtiers let out
such a yell that the Read Bird was blown off his
perch and the King's crown fell over one ear.

"What's this?" panted His Majesty, as soon
as he could make himself heard about the awful
hub-bub. "What's the meaning of this, Sixentwo?" Sixentwo was the chief of Ato's councillors and at this question the old wise man stepped
out from the crowd.

"Insurrection, Your Majesty!" explained Sixentwo calmly. "Rebellion, desertion, and de-
parture. In other words, farewell, *forever!*"

"*Forever!*" echoed Ato, straightening his crown.
"What in cheesewax are you talking about?"

"About leaving," shouted Sevenanone, Lord

50

High This and That of the realm. "We refuse to stay longer on this stuffy little island or serve a King as tiresome and unenterprising as yourself. In your whole reign you have conquered no one, made no new laws, voyages, or discoveries."

"I told you we ought to have a war," sighed Roger, who had regained his perch and was endeavoring to find the place in his book.

"War?" repeated Sevenanone, glaring fiercely at Roger while Ato ruffled up the only eight hairs he had on his head. "All he cares about is listening to your miserable croaking. All he knows is nothing, and all he does is sleep!"

"Treason!" shrieked Roger hurling his book at Sevenanone. "Down on your Octagonknees and beg His Majesty's pardon!" But the excited

Islanders paid no heed to Ato's pleas or the Read
Bird's scolding.

"We are taking the treasure, the crops, the
ship, everything but the furnishings of the castle!" sniffed Fourandfour, Treasurer of the Island. "And now, perhaps you will bestir yourself, old pudding. As for us, we go to open up
a new country, to find a king worthy of our
mettle."

"Here! Hear!" applauded the Octagonesians,
and picking up their guns, mops, rods and other
implements, they tramped scornfully from the
royal presence. Rushing to the window, Ato
presently saw them marching down to his splendid ship the *Octopus*, heavily laden with the
island's crops and treasure, the women and children skipping joyfully behind.

"Dee—serted! By ginger!" puffed His
Eightjesty, limping back to the throne, for the
cook had dropped his iron frying pan on his foot
in the course of the excitement. "Dear, dear
and dear! I hope they'll not run into any storms
or hurricanes. And what are *we* to do, my good
Roger? What of us?" While the King was looking
out the window, the Read Bird had flown to the
top shelf of the bookcase, and coming back with
a huge green volume began hurriedly flipping
over the pages. *Maxims for Monarchs*, was the
title of the green book.

"When all is lost, there is nothing more to
lose, no need for worry and nothing to be done,"
read Roger impressively.

"Very good," agreed Ato, folding his hands resignedly on his stomach. "Then I shall do nothing, my dear Roger, and while I am doing nothing, you may proceed with the story." Both pretended not to hear the rattle of chains and the shouts of the rebels as the King's ship got under way. Both pretended not to notice the silence that presently came creeping into the castle and smothering down upon them. The ticking of the clock seemed unusually loud and insistent, and without knowing why, Roger lowered his voice almost to a whisper and the King, when he thought the Read Bird was not looking, stole frequent and apprehensive glances out the window. Perhaps an hour had passed in this uneasy fashion when, to the consternation of the two castaways, there came a thunderous knock at the castle door. The Read Bird dropped his book, and Ato, blinking his eyes, half rose from his throne.

"There is nobody on the island, and yet somebody is without!" puffed Ato nervously.

"Yes, but it is not the King's place to answer the door," chattered Roger, regaining his balance with some difficulty. "Remember, even though you are deserted, you are still the King!"

"That's so!" Greatly relieved, Ato sank back among his cushions. "Er—how does the King behave under such conditions?" he inquired tremulously, as the first knock was followed b by a series of blows, kicks and furious rattles. Before Roger could find the proper place or an-

swer in *Maxims for Monarchs*, the door gave way with a great crash and splintering of timbers and tremendous footsteps came thumping along the passageway.

"I—I always said if you let matters alone they would settle themselves," stuttered Roger, hopping down on the King's shoulder and trying to hide behind his back.

"V-very unsettling, I call this," coughed Ato, reaching up to straighten his crown. "Kindly take your wing out of my eye so I can see what's coming."

"What do you see?" quavered Roger, burrowing deeper into the King's cloak. Ato was too startled to answer, and taking a frightened peek, Roger saw a monstrous seaman striding toward the throne. A gust of salt wind seemed to move along with him and his very hair and clothes seemed alive with it. The fellow's skin was red and rough, his beard and hair, showing under the tightly bound red kerchief, was bleached light yellow by the sun. He wore enormous gold earrings, his blue eyes glittered, his white teeth shone, but for all that there was something fresh and hearty about him that the cutlass swinging from his belt and the blunderbuss held in his hand could not dispel.

"Hah!" roared the intruder in a voice that set the curtains blowing. "Is there no one to announce me? Must I break a few heads as well as doors here? *Hah!*"

"Hah—hahnounce the visitor, Roger," directed Ato in a faint wheeze.

"A pirate!" groaned Roger leaning over to whisper in the King's ear. "I feared this. I feared this. No honest traveller wears his handkerchief on his head." The straightening up, Roger cried out in a voice he tried to keep steady, "Name, please, and business, if respectable!" Roger's voice was almost as faint as the King's but he managed an air of importance and dignity nevertheless.

"*Salt!*" boomed the seaman, "Sam-u-e-l Salt, the pirate, an exceedingly *irate* pirate," he finished, winking wickedly at the Read Bird.

"Salt, Samuel Salt, you are in the presence of Ato the Eighth, King of the Octagon Isle. And have you come to call, Master Salt?"

"To *call?*" exclaimed the pirate, slapping his thigh so that his scimitar rattled fearfully. "What should I call? Fish, oranges, spinach or potatoes? Do you take me for a peddler? Hah!"

"Hah, hah! No, indeed," laughed Ato feebly. "May I present Roger, my Royal Read Bird, Master Salt?"

"Roger? Good!" The pirate stared hard at Roger who, it must be confessed, was trembling like a reed by this time. "Good! He shall flap at my mast head before night. Every pirate should have a jolly Roger. What? Now then, mates, trot out your men and treasure. I have come to pillage and plunder, to loot, sack, enslave, and destroy and to knock eight bells out of everybody. Hah!" With scimitar uplifted Samuel Salt strode nearer, and Roger, falling upon the fat volume on the floor beside the throne, began frantically to turn the pages. As Roger continued to look desperately through *Maxims for Monarchs*, Ato rose and holding up his hand in a really regal manner, spoke.

"Stop!" commanded the King in a dignified voice. "You will find eight bells in the Octagon tower, but I am sorry to disappoint you about the rest. There is no one on this island but this honest bird and myself. My subjects have deserted me, Captain Salt, and gone off with my ship and all the treasure."

"Deserted!" yelled the pirate, in such a savage voice that Roger scrambled under the throne and put his head under his wing. "Well, I'm the son of a sun fish if we both aren't in the same jolly boat."

The King of the Octagon Isle

"But there isn't any boat," explained Ato, shuddering slightly as the pirate's scimitar touched his knee.

CHAPTER 6
The Story of Samuel Salt

"NO boat!" cried the pirate hoarsely. "How do you suppose I reached this island, old Eighty Pate? Look yonder! There lies my ship, the *Crescent Moon*, as fine a boat as ever rammed a sloop or sank a merchantman. My ship—and not a man, mouse or biscuit aboard her," he finished, in a depressed whisper.

"You mean you're alone?" piped the Read Bird, sticking out the end of his bill. The pirate nodded gloomily, at which Roger scurried from beneath the throne and hopped up on Ato's shoulder.

"You give him a clout in the middle while I drop this book on his head," urged the Read Bird under his breath. "Come on now, all together!"

"No, wait!" begged Ato, who had been eyeing the pirate with more interest than alarm. "I believe he's going to tell us his story."

"Story!" hissed Roger furiously. "Can't you think of anything but stories? Better do as I say or it will be the last story Your Majesty will ever hear." The pirate, lost in thought, seemed not to notice this whispered conversation, but as Roger, extremely displeased and ruffled, began to fan himself vigorously with his tail, Samuel Salt looked up.

"It happened on a Wednesday," he began moodily. "We had just put in at Elbow Island. That's where I hide my treasure and rest between voyages. I was in the green cavern studying over a map of Ozamaland, which I meant to explore, when Peggo the Red, Binx the Bad, and all the rest of the band crowded in on me and said they were leaving."

"Leaving?" Ato leaned forward, his eyes snapping with interest and sympathy. "How curious. And did they really leave you?"

"Flat!" said the pirate glumly. "I think it was Binx who banged me with the oar. But when I waked up they were gone, all the treasure was gone, all the food and supplies were gone and my second best ship, the *Sea Lion* was gone. Now, Elbow Island, mates, is a barren reef where nothing grows but rocks, and there being nought to eat and little water in the casks, I boarded the *Crescent Moon* and sailed east by nor'east till I sighted this island. Here I meant to help myself to what I needed, seize enough men to man my ship and go after those thieving rascals and bring 'em back in irons."

"Well," questioned Ato breathlessly, for he was more interested in the pirate's story than in his own safety, "why didn't you?" The pirate gazed at the King for a full moment in a stunned silence and then burst into a hearty roar.

"Hah, hah!" boomed Samuel Salt hilariously, "You're a fine King, asking me why I don't steal your treasure and enslave your men. Besides didn't you just tell me your subjects had gone off with everything of value? That's why I said we were in the same boat, old fellow. You've been robbed and deserted. I've been robbed and deserted. So, you see, we're shipmates and I couldn't treat you rough if I wanted to, could I, now?"

"No," Ato put his fingertips together and regarded his visitor thoughtfully, "I suppose not. But I suspect you of having a kind heart, Captain Salt." The pirate winced and turned red as an August moon.

"Hah, hah! You're a fine pirate!" teased the Read Bird, rocking back and forth on his perch.

"Why did your men leave you?" queried the King, shaking his finger reprovingly at Roger.

"Well," admitted Samuel Salt, shuffling his

feet uncomfortably, "to tell the truth, they claimed I wasn't rough enough either in my talk or actions. Come to think of it, they only made me chief because I was clever at navigating. Now, I hold that once you've taken a ship and stowed her valuables, you should let the passengers and crew go. But Binx was all for planking 'em. And I wouldn't stand for it."

"Planking 'em?" Ato shuddered in spite of himself. "You mean shoving them into the sea, Captain Salt?" Samuel nodded ruefully and the Read Bird rolled up his eyes in horror.

"Then," continued the pirate in a grieved voice, "as we'd been pirating a long time and had accumulated considerable gold and treasure, I was planning to do a little exploring on my next voyage, a little exploring, honest discovery, and collecting of specimens. That's what I really like," he informed them earnestly.

"And they hit you with an oar just for that," mused the King, rubbing his chin reflectively. "Just because you like exploring and didn't talk rough enough. Dear, dear and dear, how dreadfully unreasonable."

"It seems to me you talked pretty rough when you stepped in here," sniffed Roger, ruffling up his neck feathers. "How about that, Mr. Pirate?"

"I was practicing," admitted Samuel Salt, clearing his throat apologetically. "If I am to win back my crew I must be rough, bluff and relentless, mates."

"WHY DID YOUR SUBJECTS LEAVE?"

The Story of Samuel Salt

"And you wish to win them back?" asked Ato wonderingly.

"Of course, don't you?" Stepping a bit closer, the pirate looked earnestly at the King. "By the way, why did your subjects leave?"

"Because he likes stories better than people," chirped Roger, closing one eye. "Because he hasn't done any law-making, conquering or exploring. He's just too kind and easy-going, if you ask me, Mr. Salt. A King has to be hard, haughty and something of a rascal to get himself appreciated these days."

"I believe you're right," mused the pirate thoughtfully. "You'll have to practice being hard, mate. We'll both have to practice," blustered Samuel, tightening his belt and glaring around savagely.

"Well, you needn't practice on me," grumbled the Read Bird as Ato, following the pirate's example drew his face into a fierce and unaccustomed scowl. "How are you going to get your men back? What are you going to do and when are you going to do it?" demanded Roger, shutting his fan tail with a snap and pointing his claw severely at his master. Ato looked a trifle dashed, but the pirate, giving his belt another hitch, answered for him.

"We'll take the *Crescent Moon*, we'll pirate around a bit till we've enough supplies and men to man her, and then we'll sail after these rebels and bring them back by the necks, heels, ears and whiskers. Shiver my bones if we'll not! But first we must eat. *Hah!*" Expelling his breath in a mighty blast through his nose, the pirate patted his belt and looked inquiringly at Ato. "I'm hollow as a drum amidships!" The King, who had been listening in round-eyed admiration to the pirate, now brought his fist down with a tremendous thump on the arm of the throne.

"Vassals, bring the meat!" commanded Ato in a thunderous voice. "Varlets, fetch the fruit! Bring the bread and the pudding!"

"And make it lively or I'll give ye a taste of my belt!" bellowed Samuel Salt, rattling his blunderbuss threateningly. Then the King and the pirate exchanged pleased glances. "I guess that's telling 'em," rumbled Samuel Salt, rubbing his hands complacently together and striding up and down before the throne.

"Them?" coughed Roger, rocking backward and forward on his perch. "Ha, ha! What a waste of hard language. There's nobody below and you very well know it."

"That's so!" Completely crestfallen the King looked up at the Read Bird. "What are we to do, Roger?" he asked mournfully.

"Fetch it ourselves," answered Roger, flopping off his perch and making a bird line for the kitchen. But the kitchen, when they reached it, was in utmost confusion. Unwashed dishes were heaped on every table and chair, even spilling on to the floor, and though they searched in every chest and cupboard, they could find nothing but a small measure of flour, a pat of butter,

half a pitcher of milk and three broken eggs in a bowl. The cook had taken everything else eatable, even the mouse trap cheese, As the three stared dismally at the unappetizing collection, the kitchen door gave a sudden creak and slowly began to open.

"Hi-sst!" warned the pirate, giving the King's cloak a warning tug. "Some of your men returning. Now brace up, mate! Rough, bluff and relentless is the game and under the hatches with all hands and villains! *Hah!*" Carried away by the pirate's example, Ato caught up a bread knife and faced about, just as a small boy stepped through the doorway. Water ran in riivulets from his hair and clothing and he had evidently been through some exciting and exhausting experiences. His face was freckled and inquiring, but as he caught a glimpse of the threatening figures

on the other side of the kitchen table, he sprang back in dismay and would have taken to his heels had Roger not called out to him.

"Don't go!" twittered Roger, terribly relieved to find the enemy so small. "Don't go! They're only practicing!"

"Well, bless my buckles!" The pirate dropped his scimitar with a crash. "It's a boy! What ship spilled you, little lubber? You've had a taste of the sea, I see. Ha, ha! A joke!" Giving Ato a good-natured shove the pirate grinned so broadly that the boy stopped short and looked curiously from one to the other. "He's had a taste of the sea and for the sea. Nay, doubtless he ran off to sea to see what he could see. Ha, ha, ha!" finished Samuel Salt, laughing uproariously.

"Ha, ha!" echoed the King, putting down the bread knife, secretly delighted that the rough, bluff and relentless stuff was for the time being unnecessary.

"Shall I announce him in the usual fashion?" inquired Roger, leaning over to have a better look at the newcomer. "Name, young gentleman, and present business and past place of residence, if any?"

"My name is Peter Brown. I come from Philadelphia, in the United States. I'd like to dry off and have something to eat, if you don't mind," answered the boy, coming a step closer.

"We don't mind at all," said Ato pleasantly, "but unfortunately there's nothing to eat." He waved sorrowfully and apologetically around the disordered kitchen. "We've just been robbed and deserted," explained the King.

"Let me present His Majesty, Ato the Eighth, King of this island, and Samuel Salt the pirate,

who came to capture but stayed to defend us," put in Roger, sweeping back his head feathers with a practiced claw. "I myself am the Royal Read Bird. And now would you mind telling me what you have under your arm, Master Peter- delphia, or whatever you call yourself?"

"Just Peter," corrected the boy, with a quick smile at Roger. "I found this flask in the water when I was washed up on your beach. I don't know what's in it," he added, obligingly holding up the wicker covered bottle he had under his arm.

"Do—not—open!" puffed the pirate, leaning forward to read the water-soaked label on the strange flask. "Do—not—open! Well, what may that mean?"

CHAPTER 7
The Mysterious Flask

"DO not open." The Read Bird and the pirate repeated the phrase several more times and could not take their eyes from the mysterious bottle, but the King was much more interested in Peter.

"Tell me, boy," wheezed the fat monarch, easing himself slowly into a kitchen chair, "tell me how you happened to reach this island. Was it a shipwreck?" At the prospect of hearing another story Ato's eyes sparkled with pleasure and anticipation. Setting the flask on the table, Peter nodded so vigorously that drops of water flew in every direction.

"Hah!" The pirate looked up, his attention momentarily diverted from the flask. "A shipwreck you say? Were you rammed and sunk or blown on the rocks? Tell me that, young one."

"Yes," begged Ato, folding his hands on his stomach and benevolently regarding Peter, "start at the beginning and tell us everything about yourself."

"Well," began Peter thoughtfully, "there isn't much to tell. I live in Philadelphia with my grandfather. I'm eleven years old and go to the Blaine School and am captain of the baseball team." Ato pursed his lips and nodded understandingly, though he had no idea at all what a baseball team might be. Samuel Salt, whittling at the handle of a wooden spoon with his dagger, decided it must be a small ship. "Well, a friend of my grandfather's," went on Peter earnestly, "has a yacht and he invited us to go on a cruise, so of course we did. When we got off Cape Hatteras we struck a hurricane and the captain ordered all hands below, but I sneaked up to see what was going on and—"

"Were blown off!" chuckled the pirate, shaking the wooden spoon reprovingly at the boy.

"Yes," admitted Peter with a little shudder, "I was, and with almost all the stuff on deck. There was a big table that floated pretty well, so I climbed aboard. It was raining in torrents and thundering awfully. The waves were forty

feet, I guess, and the wind so high I couldn't
half breathe. I don't remember all that happened; I just went slamming ahead of the wind,
crashing through one wave and then another so
fast I couldn't think, and when the hurricane
finally died down it was night and I couldn't see.

I must have slept awhile, though, for when I
waked up it was morning and I saw land. So I
paddled with my feet and arms till I was close
enough to swim ashore. Floating on the water
I found this cask, so I brought it along. And
say, am I anywhere near the Land of Oz? I've
been to Oz a couple of times and it's the only
country I know where birds can talk, and everything is sort of—er—sort of—"

"What?" demanded Roger stiffly.

"Well—different," concluded Peter, with a long, interested look at Ato and the pirate. Then, sobering quickly, he sighed. "Golly! I wish I knew what has happened to grandfather."

"Your grandfather, having obeyed orders, is probably safe aboard ship. I wouldn't worry about him," advised Samuel Salt slowly. "As to latitude and longitude, you are at present on Ato's Island and there's a lot of geozify between here and the Land of Oz: the Nonestic Ocean, Ev, and the Deadly Desert. I've never been to Oz myself, not caring much for inland places, but I've heard enough about it. We could set you down on the coast of Ev, though, and then you might find some way to reach Oz by yourself."

"Oh, could you, would you?" breathed Peter, glancing eagerly from the pirate to the King. "Gee, that would be great! Have you a ship? Are you sailing soon?"

"We're going to do a bit of pirating," explained Roger importantly. "Then we're going to find his crew," the Read Bird waved his claw at Samuel Salt, "his crew and our men, and bring 'em back in irons." In quick jerky sentences, Roger told how Ato and the pirate had been robbed and deserted, how Samuel, sailing from Elbow Island to find himself a new crew, had come to the Octagon Isle and finding the King in the same plight as himself, had decided to help him.

"You see, Peter," finished the Read Bird mournfully, "both these fellows were deserted because they were kind and easy-going, which should be a terrible example to you, my boy. Never be kind and easy-going!"

"He's only just come, so he won't be going easy or any other way, at least not until we find something to eat," observed the pirate cheerfully. "Food, mates! What we require most and foremost is food!"

Peter had been so interested in Roger's story that he had almost forgotten how wet and famished he was. Now suddenly reminded of the fact, he glanced hungrily around the kitchen, his quick eyes coming to rest on the pitcher of milk, the flour, the butter, and the bowl of eggs.

"Why, there's food," cried Peter, licking the salt water from him lips. "We'll make us some pancakes."

"P-pancakes?" exclaimed the pirate, his whiskers quivering with eagerness. "What are p-pancakes?"

"You mean to stand there and tell me you've never eaten pancakes?" cried Peter incredulously. "Why, pancakes are flapjacks, and any scout can make flapjacks."

"You mustn't expect much assistance from these two," put in the Read Bird slyly. "They've never done a stroke of work in their lives, I fancy."

"There, there, Roger," muttered the King, as Peter began mixing the milk and flour and beating up the eggs. "It *will* be a bit awkward without the cook and bodyguards, and how I shall dress without some help I cannot imagine!"

"Oh, you'll get used to it," sniffed Peter in a matter-of-fact voice. "It's more fun doing things for yourself anyway."

"I believe you're right!" boomed the pirate, sweeping all the clutter of dishes from one end of the table with his scimitar. "And how do we eat these pot cakes, boy, with fist, fork or fingers?"

"Forks," grinned Peter, tasting the batter critically. "They're hot, you know." Darting over to the stove, Peter gave the fire a poke and soon the kitchen was full of the nose-tickling fragrance of griddle cakes. Samuel Salt, with surprising quickness, set the table; Roger after a long search in the pantry found a can of maple syrup, and presently they all sat down to as satisfying and merry a meal as had ever been eaten in the castle.

"You're going to be a great help to us, Peter," sighed Samuel, spearing another pancake with his scimitar. "Stick with me, little lubber, and I'll make an able-bodied seaman and an honest pirate of you yet. How would you like to ship as cabin boy and mate of the *Crescent Moon?*"

"Fine!" beamed Peter. "Just fine!" He smiled up at the burly pirate.

"And what will you make of *him?*" inquired Roger, pointing a claw at Ato.

"Cook and coxswain!" answered the pirate promptly. "And you, my bully bird, shall be lookout and take your turn with the watches."

"All that?" marvelled the Read Bird, preening

his feathers self-consciously. Ato looked rather thoughtful as Samuel continued to enlarge upon their duties at sea, but Roger, settling on his shoulder, assured him that there was a cook book in the pantry, and that he himself would read off the recipes and help with the vegetables, and thus encouraged, Ato became not only resigned but positively excited over his new position aboard the *Crescent Moon*. Much refreshed and heartened they all jumped up and began to make immediate plans for leaving the island.

Peter, having nothing of his own to pack, helped Ato select the royal garbs best suited to a sea voyage. Roger flew back and forth between the castle and the ship with the fat volumes from the King's library. Samuel Salt, finding an old fishing rod behind the door set out for the beach to catch, as he jocularly put it, some supper and breakfast for the crew. In the excitement of getting off, the cask Peter had brought ashore was almost forgotten. On his final trip through the kitchen, the boy caught sight of it standing on the table, and tucking it hurriedly under one arm ran down to join the others in the jolly-boat. They had made several trips between the island and the *Crescent Moon*, but this was the last.

"Hah!" chuckled the pirate, as Peter hoisted himself into the boat. "I see you've brought the mysterious bottle. Let's open it before we start, just to try our luck."

"Maybe it'll explode," objected Peter, shaking the cask dubiously, "or let something out that we'd rather not see. Besides, it says: 'Do not open.' "

"That's so," pondered the pirate, pulling vigorously at the oars, "but the question is, who says it?" The Read Bird, from his perch on Ato's shoulder, stared long and curiously at the cask, then opening *Maxims for Monarchs* perused it for a few moments in silence.

"Nobody shall say 'No' to the King," mumbled Roger presently. "Let Ato open the bottle."

"Ah, no!" begged Peter, hugging the cask to his chest. "Let's wait!" He could not bear the thought of anything that would delay their sailing. The *Crescent Moon*, lying at anchor with her high forward deck, her gleaming masts and great pirate figurehead, seemed to Peter the

grandest boat a boy ever shipped in, and he could
scarcely wait to get aboard and under way. The
King, for his part, was not at all anxious to open
the cask, so nothing more was said of the matter
and soon they were all climbing the rope ladder
dangling down the side of the *Crescent Moon*—
all except Roger, who flew easily aboard. In an
astonishingly short time, Samuel Salt with such
help as Peter, Roger and Ato could give him,
had hoisted sail and anchor and pointed his ship
into the wind. Peter, hanging eagerly over the
rail as the *Crescent Moon* plunged her nose into
the first wave and rose grandly to meet the second, took a long trembling breath. *Away!* They
were off and away and the voyage really begun.
Who knew what strange places and people they
would be seeing—conquering for that matter,
for had he not shipped as a pirate? A pirate, by
ginger! What would his grandfather say to that?
Feeling in his pocket he drew out his scout knife,
the only weapon he possessed, and looked at it
rather doubtfully. Samuel Salt, whistling light-
heartedly at the wheel, seemed to read Peter's
thoughts.

"There's an extra scimitar and some other
gear in the cabin," he called gaily. "Help yourself, young one, and then come back and I'll
show you how to take a turn here at the wheel."
Without waiting for a second invitation, Peter
rushed down to the pirate's cabin, and when he
returned he sported Samuel Salt's second best
scimitar and sword and a dashing red bandana.

The slap of the scimitar against his knee gave him great confidence and courage, and feeling ready for anything and bold enough to capture a whole ship single handed, Peter presented himself for inspection.

"Hah!" exclaimed Samuel Salt, eyeing him approvingly. "You're a better pirate than I am, my boy. But a good pirate never gets anywhere," he continued, giving the wheel several quick turns as Peter dropped on a coil of rope beside him. "We must be rough, bluff and relentless. *Hah!*"

"Do you think we'll overtake a vessel soon, Captain Salt?" asked Peter, squinting happily out toward the sky line.

"Maybe, yes, maybe, no! Can't tell! That's what makes the sea what it is—exciting." Taking a pipe and some tobacco from his pocket, the pirate lighted it briskly and grinned sociably down at Peter. Peter nodded understandingly, for flying under that great cloud of canvas straight toward the setting sun anything seemed possible, and was possible. Roger had gone below to arrange his books. Ato was investigating his new quarters and presently an excited voice came floating up from the galley.

"Sam, Sam-u-e-l! How do you get the feathers off these fish?" bellowed Ato.

"Sam?" blustered the Pirate, puffing out his cheeks and turning quite red. "Wha'd'ye think of that, lad? Plain Sam to the captain! Plain Sam-u-e-l! *Hah!* Ah, well!" His expression grew milder. "After all, he's a King and if a King can't call a pirate 'Sam,' what good is a crown?"

"And he's never been a cook before," Peter reminded him, as Ato came lumbering cautiously across the deck, a slippery fish held high in each hand.

"What do you do to these?" panted Ato, facing the pirate in frank bewilderment.

"Maybe you pare them," sighed Samuel Salt in a dreamy voice, "or singe them, like fowl. Oh, just boil them in their jackets," he finished, with a careless wave of his hand.

"Ho! Ho!" roared Peter, bending nearly double. "It's plain to be seen you've never cleaned a fish in your lives. Ho! Ho! It's lucky I'm with you on this voyage. Come along, King, I'll fix 'em for you!" And remembering he was cabin boy as well as mate, Peter went below to help Ato prepare the pirates' supper.

CHAPTER 8
"Land, Ho!"

A LL night and all morning the *Crescent Moon* under full sail had flown before the wind. And, short handed as they were, her crew under the capable direction of Samuel Salt managed famously. The pirate had set up a sturdy perch before the wheel so that Roger, too, could take his turn at steering, but the Read Bird much preferred post as lookout high in the forward mast. Peter, though his fingers were blistered and torn from his struggle with the sail ropes, was happier than he had ever been in his life; and the

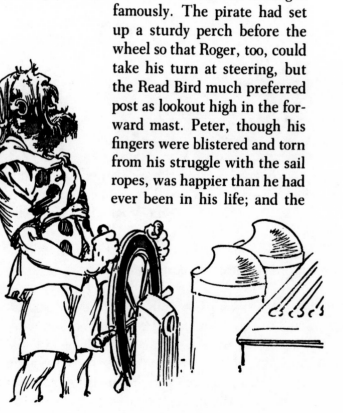

same might be said of the King, for Ato had shed
all his royal regalia and was dressed in an old
shirt belonging to Binx the Bad, and a pair of
short white trousers he had found in the fo'castle. His crown hung on a nail beside the stove
and his bald head was rakishly covered with one
of Samuel's silk handkerchiefs. Already a rough
beard had begun to show on his Majesty's chin,
giving to his mild octagon countenance quite a
wild and dangerous appearance.

"Man! He looks more like a pirate than the
captain!" chuckled Peter, as the ship's cook waved
cheerily to him from the galley. Though Peter
had been aboard many boats in his short life he
had never been on one like the *Crescent Moon*.
The pirate's ship was a three masted square-
rigged sailing vessel, speedy and beautiful. She
carried four guns, two on each side of the round
house and stowed beneath decks was enough
ammunition to sink a fleet. On his times off
duty—and there were precious few of these—
Peter, mounted on one of the port guns, anxiously scanned the Nonestic Ocean for signs of
a ship. He secretly longed for the first encoun-
ter, and each time he looked up at the pirate's
black pennant fluttering defiantly from the
masthead, his heart would pound with excitement. Ato's colors floated just below and the
Octopus with its eight serpent-like arms, the
royal insignia of the Octagon Isle, on its sea
green background, looked almost as threatening
as the skull and bones. All four adventurers

were comfortably quartered in the captain's cabin, their belongings tidily stowed away. Peter, having nothing but the flask, had shoved the strange bottle beneath his berth, and there was so much to see and do that he promptly forgot it. Carelessly and dangerously it slid backward and forward with the motion of the ship.

"Will you be terribly, fearfully angry when you overtake your men?" asked Peter, who was standing close to the pirate, ready to take his turn at the wheel.

"Terribly," answered Samuel Salt, showing all his teeth in a dazzling smile. But he said it so calmly and looked so cheerful that Peter was unconvinced.

"What do you say when you're mad?" asked the boy thoughtfully. At this point the Read Bird, who had been listening to the conversation with great interest, decided to find out, and dropped the book he was reading on the pirate's head with great force and suddenness.

"Bless my buckles!" Letting go of the wheel with one hand and rubbing his head with the other, Samuel looked upward. "Bless my boots, what's wrong with you?"

"Ho, ho, ho!" roared Roger, fluttering down to the deck. "Nothing is wrong with me but something's terribly wrong with you, Master Salt. Boots and buckles! Ha, ha! Is that the worst you can do? What a dangerous fellow you are, Samuel."

"I expect you're right," sighed the pirate, still

ruefully rubbing his head. "I can never grow sufficiently angry nor work myself up into a rage. I'll have to practice, bless my boots, to practice, that's what! Try me again, Roger, that's a good bird." At this, Peter, who had been sadly disappointed at the pirate's outburst, brightened and waited expectantly as Roger climbed into the rigging. Now perhaps the Read Bird flung his book with unnecessary violence this time, or perhaps it hit Samuel on the same place. But however that mey be, the result was immediate and terrifying. With a yell that lifted Peter's hair and Roger's feathers, the pirate flung up his hands.

"Shiver my liver!" bawled Samuel shaking his fists at Roger. " Shiver my liver and shatter my shins, I'll goosewing your topsails for this!" He took a quick step toward the mast. "Come down

83

from there, you long-billed villain, you shall hang from the yard arm and dry in the sun. Hah-aaah!" With another yell Samuel looked up at the Read Bird, and Roger, thoroughly frightened, spread both wings and started out to sea while Peter ducked behind a coil of rope.

"What's all this? What's all this?" panted Ato, running heavily across the deck. "What's all this noise and stamping?"

"Ho! Ho! Yo! Ho!" roared the pirate. "I've convinced them this time that I can get mad. Come back, mate! I was only practicing."

"Come back!" echoed Peter, straightening up a little shamefacedly and pretending he had not been at all alarmed. "Come on back, Roger. He was only fooling." The Read Bird circled over the ship several times before he could make up his mind and then rather uncertainly he dropped down on the deck.

"Well, mates, was that better?" With his hands on his hips Samuel stared from one to the other and then with an uproarious chuckle grasped the wheel.

"Gosh, yes," shuddered Peter, shaking his head to get the sound of the pirate's roars out of his ears. "If you shout like that you'd even scare a giant. Say, I tell you what! Whenever we meet a ship or sight an island, Roger can drop a book on your head."

"Not me!" quavered the Read Bird, flying up on Ato's shoulder. "Let some one else set off the fireworks." Anxious to change the subject he reached down and took the volume the King had under his arm and opened it hurriedly.

"First you take two eggs," read Roger in a rather shaky voice, for the book was a cook book, "take two eggs and—"

"Does it say there whom we shall take them from, mate?" asked Samuel, grinning amiably at the Read Bird.

"Oh, what's the good of a cook book when there's nothing to cook?" mourned Ato, flopping down on an overturned fire bucket. "Eight bells, Samuel, and not a bite on the boat. Not even a fish fin!"

"Well, we've plenty of water and that's something," answered the pirate, "and we'll pass an island or a ship soon, never fear. Go aloft, Roger, old lubber, and see what's in the wind."

"Aye, aye, sir!" Touching his forehead respectfully with his claw, Roger, still uneasy at memory of the pirate's dreadful threats, fairly flew to obey. Almost at once he let out a piercing squall.

"Land! Land, ho!" shrilled the Read Bird, pointing toward the west. Rushing over to the rail, Peter, squinting up his eyes, almost immediately made out a large dot on the sky line.

"Oooh!" breathed Pete. "It's an island! Golly, I hope it's inhabited! I hope there's plenty of treasure and gold!"

"I'd rather have a roast duck, or an omelet,"

wheezed Ato, with a wistful hitch of his belt.
"Are we going to capture everybody, Sammy, or
just enough to man the ship?"

"Well, that," answered the pirate, expertly
bringing the ship about, "that depends!"

"Oh, pshaw! Now you're being polite again,"
exclaimed Pete impatiently. "Let's be regular
pirates, capture everybody and take everything.
Golly! There's a castle!" At this the King, almost
as interested as Peter, came to lean beside him
on the rail. The island, as they came nearer,
exceeded even Peter's expectations. Its cottages
and castle, glittering in the noonday sunshine,
seemed at first glance to be constructed entirely
of jewels, but as Samuel eased the *Crescent.Moon*
into a long lagoon they discovered that the island
was of some strange coral formation and all its
houses and buildings were made of brightly pol-

"Land, Ho!"

ished shell. Floating from the castle's transparent turret was a pearly pennant bearing two words.

SHELL CITY

"Shell City!" marvelled Peter, with a little gasp of admiration. "Ginger! I wonder what kind of people live here."

"A lot of crabs, most likely," predicted Roger gloomily. "A lot of crabs who'll pinch and nip the ears off you! I think I will take a book ashore," he added in a lower voice. "If there's any fighting to be done, it's safer for Samuel to be mad." Peter nodded his approval, and tightening the belt that held his pistols ran to help the pirate lower the jollyboat.

CHAPTER 9
Shell City

"NOW, mates," cautioned Samuel Salt earnestly, as the jollyboat grounded on the shining beach, "rough, bluff and relentless is what we're going to be. Rough, bluff and relentless, remember!"

Peter and Ato nodded grimly and the Read Bird, riding jauntily on the King's shoulder, tightened his hold on his book and cackled nervously. Instead of sand, the beach was formed of sharp, tiny shells, and along the shore and surrounding each cottage tall palm trees with glittering shell bark waved their green fronds in the warm breeze. Perched on a roof Peter saw a company of turtles, and just as he nudged Samuel they spread wide white wings and flew away.

"Mother of pearl!" gasped the pirate, squinting up at the sun. "They're doves, turtledoves, mates. How would you like a turtle shell on your back, old bird?" Samuel winked broadly at Roger.

"How would you like a cocoanut shell on your head?" inquired the Read Bird saucily. "Get on, Master Salt, get on! Remember we came here on business and I crave food!"

"Right!" agreed the pirate, grinning at Roger. "Quite right!" And without stopping to admire the curious shell dwellings, and without encountering a single person they hurried toward the castle.

"I guess all the natives sleep in the daytime," ventured Peter, remembering what he had read of tropical islands. But as they reached the castle itself, out backed the King and Queen of Shell City, and such a company as Peter had never seen in his whole mortal life. I can best describe these curious islanders by telling you they were Shellbacks. At first glance Peter thought they were enormous turtles but when they faced about, and this they did almost immediately, he discovered that they were tall, finely formed men and women, richly and elegantly dressed but firmly encased in hard brown shells.

"Hish! Hash! Hosh!" observed the King, languidly tipping his shell crown.

"Squish! Squash! Squosh!" added the Queen, extending her right hand graciously.

"Boiled plain, or mashed with butter?" inquired Roger, who had been reading up in the cook book and was hungry enough to eat even squash.

"They're talking shell," muttered Samuel Salt out of one side of his mouth. "A hard language, or I miss my guess! But they seem polite and friendly, so we'd better not do any fighting, mates. That is, not yet."

"Certainly not," agreed Ato, fumbling at the button of his shirt collar and wishing he had stopped to shave. "Perhaps they'll invite us to lunch, Sammy." The King and Queen continued to address the visitors in their strange language, and Peter, listening with lively interest, decided it sounded not unlike the swish and murmur of the sea. Just as he was wondering how he would make these singular rulers understand that he and his companions were very hungry, and just as Roger, muttering with impatience, began to circle over Samuel's head with his book, a happy thought struck Peter.

"Does Your Majesty speak Ozish?" asked the boy, suddenly remembering that Ozish was the same as English and spoken in all the fairy countries he had visited so far.

"Why, surely," replied the King, with a little sigh of relief, for he, too, was growing discouraged with the conversation. "Are you from the Land of Oz, Soft-back? I've heard of Oz many

THEY WERE ELEGANTLY DRESSED SHELLBACKS

times, though I've never been there myself. Humph! Gerumph! So you come from the Land of Oz?" With round eyes he stared at his visitors.

"Well, not exactly," explained Peter, anxious not to get into a long discussion. "You see, we came on a ship."

"A ship!" cried the King, clasping his hands delightedly. "Why, then you're shipsies. Shipsies, my dear! Shipsies!" The Queen smiled and showed all her small pearly teeth, while the King fairly bubbled over with interest and curiosity— all of which made Peter and the pirates exceedingly uneasy. How were they to fall upon and capture people so disarmingly pleasant and so persistently polite? But Roger was not bothering his head about such fine points of etiquette. Roger was hungry.

"Is there anything to eat on this island?" croaked the Read Bird hoarsely. "Is there any food in your castle, King?"

"Konk!" corrected His Majesty grandly. "I am Konk of the Shellbacks and this is the Quink."

"Ha, ha!" Roger laughed discreetly behind his claw. "Well, Konk, we've come to conquer you, old fellow, but first we must eat." Ato and the pirate frowned warningly at the Read Bird, but the Konk seemed not in the least offended by his speech.

"To konker us," he mused, rubbing his chin thoughtfully. "Well, that will be nice." To tell the truth the old Shellback had never been conquered in his life and had no idea what Roger was talking about. After a few more remarks upon the subject he graciously motioned for them to enter the castle. Floors, walls, furniture, everything was constructed of shell—shell, lovely and lustrous and iridescent as pearl. As the Shellbacks were not constructed for sitting down there were no chairs, and in the gleaming dining hall the table was shoulder high, so that Peter had to stand on a small chest to reach the board at all. And as long as he lived Peter remembered that curious company and that strange, dreadful repast.

Luncheon was served on great shining shells, and as the first course was set down before them the voyagers exchanged puzzled and uneasy glances. It consisted of six perfectly empty clam shells, which the Shellbacks contentedly munched as if they had been crackers. The Konk seemed slightly annoyed when none of his guests ate the clam shells but nodded encouragingly as the second course was brought in. But this proved to be even worse, for it was sea water soup with live fish and snails, served in small glass aquariums. Peter shuddered and even the pirate winced as the Shellbacks calmly swallowed down live fish and snails and ladled up spoonful after spoonful of the bitter salt water. As they pushed back their aquariums, Roger put his head under his wing, and the Konk's annoyance deepened. By the time the third course arrived the Shellbacks were scowling and muttering disagreeably. Looking down hopefully and hungrily, Peter

saw a nicely cracked lobster shell, two broken eggshells and a heap of pea shells. The Konk, after liberally sprinkling his lunch with sand from a sand shaker, looked sternly at his guests. The pirate, politest of them all, was making a pretense of eating a lobster claw. Ato and Peter after one look pushed back their plates, and Roger, emitting a feeble groan, put his head under his wing again. On a side table Peter caught a glimpse of dessert, half cocoanut shells filled with peach skins, banana skins and walnut shells.

"Well," demanded the Konk, angrily meeting Peter's dismayed glance, "what's wrong, Softback?"

"Nothing," answered Peter sulkily, growing a little angry himself at the Konk's insolent stare. "Nothing's wrong, but we can't eat shells. They're not our kind of food."

"Can't?" shouted the ruler of Shell City, growing red as a lobster. "Who dares to say can't to the Konk? How do you expect to grow shells unless you eat them?"

"We don't expect to grow shells," put in Ato calmly. "We—"

"Don't expect to grow shells!" howled the Konk, now quite beside himself with anger. "Then why did you take shelter on our island? You can't stay here without shells! Snipper Snapper! Seize these shipsies, throw them in the watery dungeons and keep them there until their shells grow. They shell learn to eat shells! Clam shells, cocoanut shells, oyster shells, lobster shells, eggshells and—"

"Bombshells!" exploded the pirate, swallowing the lobster claw and jumping furiously to his feet, for Roger, seeing something must be done, had dropped a book hard on his head. "Bombshells!" roared Samuel again. Thoroughly aroused he banged his fists so hard on the table that the shell plates bounced and skipped.

"Shiver your liver!" prompted Peter, giving Samuel a little shove as Snipper Snapper dashed toward them.

"Aye! And shiver their shells, too!" rumbled the pirate. "Come on, mates, rough, bluff and relentless now. We'll get back to our boat and give them a taste of our kind of shells. Ball, shot and bombshells. *Hah!*" Samuel's ferocious snort and glare so upset the Konk and Quink that they tumbled over backward. Then Peter saw with relief and astonishment that in this position they were perfectly harmless and helpless, rocking backward and forward on their shells and quite unable to rise.

"Quick, fellows! Push them all over," whispered Peter, as Snipper Snapper made a snatch at his sleeve. And this Ato, Peter and Samuel did so quickly and so cleverly that in two minutes there was not an islander on his feet in the whole great dining hall.

"Ha, ha, ha! They have all turned turtle!" squealed Roger gleefully. "A Konk and a Quink on the half shell, mates! Come on, Ato, let's raid the kitchen. Where there are clam shells and eggshells there must be clams and eggs. Where there are oyster shells there must be oysters. Yo, ho! What a barrel of fun!"

"Conquered without a man lost or hurt!" boasted the pirate, grinning down at the kicking, squirming Shellbacks. "And now for a few rare specimens!" Striding off, the pirate left Peter standing undecided in the midst of the overturned islanders. Then, reasoning, as Roger had done, that where there were oyster shells there might also be pearls, Peter rushed out into the royal kitchen. Trays of freshly shelled peas and nuts, bowls of fresh oysters, clams and lobster meat, and plates of fruit without skins stood about, ready to be thrown away. The cook and his helper had been quickly pushed over by Ato, and the King and Roger were busily at work packing baskets and jars with oysters, clams,

"THEY HAVE ALL TURNED TURTLE!"

pared peaches, lobster meat and a quantity of unshelled vegetables they had discovered in the pantry. With little grunts and nods of satisfaction the former ruler of the Octagon Isle fell upon the eatables, stowing them into pails and hampers as if they had been the rarest of gems. Swallowing a few raw oysters and finishing off with a banana, Peter ran into the back courtyard and there, sure enough, were his pearls—heaps, mounds, and shimmering masses of them—carelessly thrown out like paper or trash by the heedless inhabitants of the island. There were pearls enough to ransom a kingdom, a dozen kingdoms for that matter.

"Great gollywockers!" gasped the boy, and snatching two pillow cases from a line stretched across the court, he began feverishly filling them with pearls. In two hot, tiresome trips he carried them down to the jolly-boat. Each time he met one of the islanders he pushed him over and soon the air was full of their screams and outcries.

"Shell barks!" Roger mischievously called them, as he flew past Peter on his way to the *Crescent Moon* with two pails and a picnic basket.

"Where's Samuel?" called Peter, who was growing rather tired of the racket the Shellbacks were making. Roger shook his head and shrugged his feathers, but just then a long hail from the beach sent the boy scurrying down to see what the pirate had found. There stood Samuel with two plump sheldrakes he had brought down with his gun, and a great heap of shells, small crabs, mollusks and sea weed.

"Say, what do you want with that stuff?" teased Peter, as Samuel tenderly gathered up his treasures. "Why, I've got two great bags full of pearls and Ato's found enough grub to last us for days!"

"I've always been interested in conchology," answered the pirate, dreamily fingering his shells, "and the flora and fauna on this island are extremely exotic."

"Ex-whatic?" coughed Peter, wrinkling up his forehead. "Golly, Skipper, you ought to be an explorer or something like that." The pirate nodded seriously and shouldering his wild ducks sent a long "Halloo" across the island.

"We'll have to shove off if we want to catch

this wind," he observed, holding up his hand critically. "Here's Roger but I wonder what's become of our cook? Let's go up to the castle and hurry him along." Walking carefully around the fallen islanders, they made their way quickly back to the shell castle and after a long hunt found Ato in the library simply surrounded by the Konk's shell bound books.

"I thought Roger could read these to us in the long winter evenings," muttered Ato, looking up happily at them.

"But it's summer!" objected Peter with a laugh. "Oh, well, come along. I'll help you carry them." Out of the corner of his eye he saw Samuel Salt counting out some gold pieces and jewels on the library table.

"To pay for the books and supplies, I suppose," chuckled Peter to himself. "Gosh! He *is* a funny pirate! I hope he doesn't pay for the pearls for they were just plain thrown away." Catching Peter's eye, Samuel blushed guiltily and seizing a pile of books dashed out of the castle and ran all the way down to the jolly-boat. In less than an hour they were all aboard the *Crescent Moon*, outward bound. Shell City was just a sparkling dot behind them.

"Well," mused the pirate, squinting thoughtfully up at the sun, "taken all in all 'twas a pretty good haul, but maybe we should have turned those chaps over before we left."

"There were plenty of Shellbacks in the cottages to do that," answered Peter, bringing the ship cleverly into the wind, for it was his turn at the wheel. "Gosh, Skipper, we forgot to capture any able-bodied seamen."

"Ah, well," sighed the pirate, leaning back against a davit, "it's cozier as it is, Pete. No crew to quarrel and bicker over treasure. No arguments. And what good would those half shells have been on deck? One roll and toss and they'd be flat on their backs hollering for help. Of course it does keep us all hustling, but I don't know when I've enjoyed a voyage like this one."

"Me, too!" agreed Peter. "And I don't care how long it lasts, either. Mmm—mm! Roast duck! What time is it, Samuel?"

"Three bells!" boomed the pirate with a furious sniff. "Hah! Ato may be a poor King but he's certainly a rare cook." Stimulated and inspired by the appetizing whiffs from the galley, where Ato and Roger were preparing supper,

Samuel broke into an old sea chantey, beating out the measures with his pipe and singing so lustily that the very sails trembled and lifted with each line.

"Ho, storm along, my bullies!
Where the waves roll high and free;
Old Davey Jones can have his bones,
But I shall have the sea!"

"The sea!" crooned Peter cheerfully. He fixed his eye on the distant horizon and wondered what strange lands and adventures might lie beyond, whether they would be able to reach Oz, and how many of the Konk's pearls he would be able to take back to Philadelphia with him.

CHAPTER 10
Meanwhile, in Ev—

WHILE Peter and Samuel Salt, Ato, and Roger were cruising off in the *Crescent Moon*, strange enough things were happening in Menankypoo. The morning after the bucca-neers had made him chief, Ruggedo descended to find the pirates in absolute control of the city. They had already taken the gold and jewels from the treasury, ransacked the castle, and were now removing such furniture and ornaments as ap-pealed to them to their red-sailed boat in the bay. At first the Gnome King was inclined

to argue about his share of the treasure, but Clocker advised against it.

"What difference does it make?" said the slip presented by the cuckoo, as the Wise Man struck ten. "When we reach the Emerald City we will destroy these pirates anyway and then in our own good time return for the ship. The thing to do now is to humor them, humor them and bide your time." So Ruggedo, cleverly concealing his displeasure, pretended to fall in with their plans and after the pirates, under the direction of Binx and Peggo, had stored all the stuff worth taking aboard the *Sea Lion*, he called a council in the Yellow Courtyard.

"The journey to Oz," began the Gnome King, who had exchanged the crown of Menankypoo for the knotted kerchief of the pirates, "the journey to Oz is long and tedious, and before we undertake the trip, you who are seamen must learn to march and drill and stand up under the hardships of land fighting. So fall in and we'll do a practice stretch up the beach. Fall in and I'll make you the finest fighting seamen Oz has ever known—regular Oz marines," boasted Ruggedo, swelling out his chest.

"Ha, Ha!" rumbled Binx, winking at Peggo. "Listen to the little fighting cock, will you? But we have other plans, my hearty, and I for one am going to spend the day as I please, eating, arguing and sleeping in the garden. How about you, mates?"

"Aye! Aye! That suits us," yelled the pirates,

and grinning and nudging one another they began to move off.

"Stop!" shouted the Gnome King, by this time quite beside himself with anger. "How dare you talk to me like that? I am chief and captain of this band and I *command* you to fall in and march to the sea."

"You *command* us?" exclaimed Peggo, grinning down at the sputtering gnome. "Ho, ho, mates! He *commands* us! Ho! Dim my portlights, that's too good!" Then, as Ruggedo began to stamp, yell and wave his arms, the pirate gave him a good-natured push. "Oh, go catch flies," advised Peggo indulgently. "Go catch flies or frogs or knit yourself a sweater. We made you chief so you could show us the way to Oz. When we're ready to start we'll let you know. Now run along and don't bother me." Giving Ruggedo another shove, Peggo turned on his heel and with derisive shouts and chuckles the buccaneers disappeared in the direction of the garden.

"This is all your fault," raged the Gnome King, shaking his fist at Clocker, who had stood quietly beside him during the whole performance. "We should have gone off by ourselves and never told them about Oz. Did you hear how they talked to me? To *me*, the former Metal Monarch, the present King of Menankypoo and chief of the band! Billygoats and bottlebirds, if I just had my magic belt I'd turn them to pebbles and pitch them into the sea. I'd turn them to potatoes and boil them for supper. I'd—" There seemed

105

no end to the things Ruggedo would do and with
a bored yawn the Wise Man sat down on a bench
and put his fingers in his ears. Realizing that
there was nobody to listen to him, Ruggedo finally stopped scolding and lapsed into a sullen
silence, waiting impatiently for Clocker to speak.
Clocker was not in an expecially good humor
himself, for when he did strike the cuckoo
screamed savagely eleven times and struck Ruggedo a sharp blow between the eyes. Then,
thrusting the yellow paper on the Gnome King's
long nose, like a clerk sticks a letter on a file,
it hurtled back to its little cupboard and slammed
the door. Without waiting to see how Ruggedo
would take his advice, Clocker started across
the sand. Snatching the paper from his nose,
and glaring at it with eyes that bulged with anger
and indignation, Ruggedo read:

"Come to the conjurer's cave."

Meanwhile, ın Ev—

"I'll smash that Cuckoo some day," fumed the gnome, tearing the paper into about a thousand pieces. Then, because he was afraid to remain behind and risk his life with the pirates, he stamped sulkily after the Wise Man of Menankypoo, stealing anxious glances over his shoulder now and then to make sure no one was following him. As soon as they were inside the cave, Clocker walked stiffly to one of the chests Ruggedo had tried to open and tapped three times on the lid. It raised up instantly, and leaning down Clocker pulled out a soft green hood and a heavy ebony stick. Clapping the hood on the gnome's head, he drew off and struck him a staggering blow on the chin. Ruggedo never budged nor winced. In fact he did not feel the blow at all and the ugly scowl he had been wearing all morning melted away as if by magic. Dragging off the hood he examined it carefully all over. Embroidered in the lining he found the word "Hardy-hood."

"Hardy-hood!" exulted the gnome. "Ha, ha! Now let them try any more of their nonsense. You *are* a good fellow, Clocker, and a smart one, too. What else have you there?" Darting toward the Wise Man Ruggedo was caught midway and held rigid. Clocker had raised the ebony stick and he smiled calmly and provokingly at the gnome's frightful cries and faces. As long as the Wise Man held the stick up Ruggedo found it impossible to move, but as soon as it touched the floor the spell was broken.

107

"What is it? Let me have it! Let me have it! I'll show those pesky pirates who's who and what's what!" cried the old elf vindictively. Clocker struck and thrust the stick into Ruggedo's hand at the same time and the cuckoo's yellow paper told all about the conjurer's curious treasures.

"The wearer of the Hardy-hood cannot be hurt or injured," it stated calmly. "The holder of the Standing-stick can make anyone stand 'round. It is one of the most powerful inventions of Cinderbutton, the witch. Go back and try it on the pirates."

"Why, how perfectly mellifluous!" Ruggedo rapturously hugged the ebony stick to his skinny little chest. "And how it will help us when we reach the Emerald City! You shall be well rewarded for this, my good Clocker. You shall have half the kingdom and the Patchwork Girl for a slave." Clocker, who meant to have the whole kingdom, nodded solemnly at Ruggedo and winked roguishly at himself in the mirror. Then, both conspirators wrapped themselves in the conjurer's cape and flew up the chimney.

When Peggo, stretched with the other pirates comfortably under the trees in the garden, saw Ruggedo and the Cuckoo Clock Man striding toward them, he raised up inquiringly on one elbow. But when the Gnome King in a loud voice again commanded the pirates to rise and march to the beach, Peggo jumped to his feet with a bellow of anger and gave the gnome a buffet that would have staggered an elephant. The astonishment of the pirates when it neither budged nor jarred their tiny chieftain can well be imagined. As Binx the Bad and the fifty-eight other buccaneers rushed to help Peggo, the gnome lifted the Standing-stick and not only brought them to a standstill, but rendered them as harmless as wooden soldiers. Then in a speech that sent Clocker into soundless gales of merriment, Ruggedo spoke his mind and issued his orders. The pirates were not only to obey him in every way, to march, drill and prepare for war with Oz, but they were also to address him at all times as Ruggedo the Rough, King of the Gnomes, Monarch of Menankypoo, Chief of the Band, Captain of the *Sea Lion* and Emperor of Oz!

"Understand?" roared Ruggedo in a ferocious voice. "Understand? Now then, who am I?"

109

"Ruggedo the Rough, King of the Gnomes, Monarch of Menankypoo, Chief of the Band, Captain of the *Sea Lion* and Emperor of Oz!" repeated the helpless and mortified sea robbers mournfully.

"Very well." Nodding grimly, Ruggedo, who, it must be confessed, knew kinging from the ground up, dropped the magic stick. "Fall in! Forward march!" For two hours the fierce and determined little gnome drilled his sulky and unwilling army, and he would not have stopped then had not a sudden cry from Binx called his attention to a strange vessel anchoring in the bay.

"Yo, ho! Yo, ho!" yelled Binx, forgetting all about Ruggedo for the moment. "A boat, mates! A prize! Back to the *Sea Lion* and give her the guns!"

"Halt!" cried Ruggedo, as the pirates made a dash for their small boats. "Halt! And don't forget, I'm captain here. There'll be no gun work unless I call for it."

"Cuckoo, cuckoo, cuckoo!" mocked the yellow bird, darting out of Clocker's head, for it was exactly three o'clock. And while the pirates, muttering and glowering, fell back in line, Ruggedo calmly read the Wise Man's message.

"Enlist these newcomers in your army by trick or stick," advised Clocker, "and afterward we will steal their ship and treasure." Ruggedo nodded and thrust the paper in his pocket. Then, handing the ebony stick to the Wise Man, he motioned for him to keep the pirates in order while he went down to confer with the captain of the strange boat, who was already stepping ashore. The pirate ship, which might have frightened the visitors away, was hidden behind a jutting cliff.

"Salutations and greetings!" began the stranger, as Ruggedo, looking as tall and impressive as a four foot sovereign well could, advanced to meet him. "Seeing your harbor lights from afar, and feeling they must mark a friendly country, we have anchored here to ask your advice and counsel. We are colonists from the Octagon Isle, anxious to settle in a new and progressive kingdom and serve a King who is ambitious and clever, who will forward our interests by battle and conquest and give us an opportunity to show our own bravery and skill. Does Your Excellency know of such a King or country?" Somewhat out of breath, Sixentwo, who had taken upon himself the position of captain of the *Octopus* and leader of the rebels, paused and looked earnestly at the strange figure before him.

"Go no farther!" cried Ruggedo, raising his arm impressively. "This is the country you seek, and I, its present ruler, am at this very moment preparing for war with the mighty Kingdom of Oz! Settle here!" urged Ruggedo eagerly. "Join my army and when we have conquered Oz and divided its treasure you shall have this Kingdom of Menankypoo for your own."

"Huzzah! Hurrah!" shouted the Octagon Islanders, throwing up their caps and bundles. "Eighty-eight cheers for Menankypoo and its bold little King."

"Here is a ruler worth having," cried Sevenanone boisterously, "not an old sleepy-head like Ato." Ruggedo, well-pleased and well-satisfied with the result of his speech, bowed and smiled with gratification as the Octagon Islanders continued to cheer and applaud. Then, after Sixentwo had formally accepted his offer, he invited them to make themselves at home in the cottages of his former subjects. The pirates had lodged in the castle, so the eight fishermen, the eight shopkeepers, the eight soldiers, the eight sailors, the eight artists and scholars, the eight councillors, the eight courtiers, the eight servitors, the eight musicians and the eight farmers, with their wives and their children, hastily moved their belongings from the ship to the city of Menankypoo. Some of the women remarked among themselves on the puny size and extreme ugliness of their new ruler and agreed that Ato was a much more kindly and important figure, and Octagon Isle much pleasanter and more home-like than Menankypoo.

But the men paid no attention to them and dumping down their belongings unceremoniously rushed out to drill under the capable direction of Ruggedo the Rough.

Not wishing to frighten his new recruits, the gnome had sent the pirates and Clocker back to the castle. The Wise Man could easily keep them in order with the standing stick and they were too worn out from drilling to start any serious rebellion.

If the Octagon Islanders grew troublesome he would use the stick on them, too. As long as they did what he wanted, well and good. "With this company of fighters I can start for the Emerald City any day, and Clocker has found a way to cross the desert so everything will be mellifluous and grand!"

With his wrinkled little face wreathed in smiles, the vain and ambitious little midget turned to the drilling and training of good King Ato's former subjects.

CHAPTER 11
The No Bodies

NO land had been sighted for two days but Peter found it vastly exciting skimming over the mountainous green waves of the Nonestic Ocean. There was enough to do with the sails alone to keep four or five able-bodied seamen busy, and all on board the pirate's ship worked as they had never worked before. But not for anything in the world or Oz would Peter have traded his position as cabin boy and mate on the *Crescent Moon*. Sometimes, when the sea was calm and everything shipshape,

Roger would read them stories from Ato's books or the volumes they had brought from Shell City. Sometimes Samuel Salt would tell of his many strange voyages or Peter would relate his adventures in Oz.

"It was on this very ocean that I first met the Gnome King," mused Peter, as he and Samuel were mending a sail one morning. "He was on a rocky island and I was dropped there by a balloon bird. Then there was a sea-quake and we got off the island on an old pirate ship that was thrown up from the bottom of the sea. Did you ever know Polacky, Samuel?" Samuel Salt shook his head thoughtfully.

"Well, anyway," went on Peter, "it was his ship, but it was pretty well done for, so we just drifted till we came to Ev. Then with a magic cloak of invisibility that we found on the ship, Rug flew to the Emerald City and stole back his magic belt. I followed him as quickly as I could and just as he was sending Ozma and everybody to the bottom of the Nonestic Ocean, I was lucky enough to hit him with a silence stone I had found on the pirate ship. So of course he couldn't say another word. The Wizard made him visible and that was that! Wonder what he's doing now? Boy, he was a bad one!"

"What happened the next time you came to Oz?" inquired Ato, who was sitting on a pile of life preservers, shelling peas.

"Oh, last time I met Jack Pumpkinhead and an Iffin and we flew over the whole country on

its back and captured the Baron of Baffleburg," explained Peter carelessly. "And, man! What do you think I found? A magic dinner bell. All you had to do was ring it and a slave would bring you a tray full of wonderful food."

"That would be a right handy thing to have on a voyage," sighed Ato, wiping his royal brow on the sleeve of his ragged shirt. "We've about done with the stuff we brought from Shell City, Samuel, and there's nothing for dinner but wilted peas and bad peaches."

"Sounds all right to me," said Samuel Salt, looking cross-eyed as he threaded his needle. "Anyway, we'll be heading in somewhere soon. Ahoy, Roger! Anything ahead?" Roger, who for the present was steersman, shook his head without looking around.

"Water, water everywhere, and not a sign
    of land,
Oh, for a teas, oh for a teas, a teaspoonful
    of sand!"

croaked the Read Bird gloomily. Though used
to flying, Roger had suffered untold inconveni-
ences from the rocking of the *Crescent Moon* and
was wistfully looking for an island.

"Bird!" yawned Samuel Salt, stretching his
arms luxuriously up over his head, "bird, you're
bilious!"

"Buffalo Billious!" teased Peter, winking at
the King. "Are we heading for Ev, Skipper, or
straight out to sea?"

"Well," admitted Samuel, "I figured that my
men would be likely to stick to the open sea and
Ato's subjects would make for the mainland. So
first we'll cruise around and try to pick up my
ship and then we'll head in for shore and find
his."

"I don't believe his subjects would know him
now," observed Peter, looking enviously at the
King's long beard. "Gee, I wish I could grow
whiskers."

"Nonsense!" grumbled Ato, getting heavily to
his feet. "You can grow whiskers when you're
too old to do anything else. I'd trade my beard
for your nimble legs any day in the week. But
say, do I really look different, Samuel?"

"Hah! Hoh!" roared the pirate, his eyes travelling from the sunburned, whiskered face of

117

the King to the shabby toes of an old pair of sea boots the cook had found in a chest. "Not only different but better! Your own grandmother wouldn't know you, Ato."

"And you're different, too," crowed Peter, pointing mischievously at Samuel Salt. "And when you spring on your men all that new language we've been practicing they'll step pretty lively, or I'm a tin soldier."

"Do you really think so, Pete?" The pirate, who had been faithfully practicing his rough, bluff and relentless role, blushed with pleasure. "What was that last bit we decided on?" he mused meditatively.

"Avast and belay!" Peter reminded him delightedly. "Avast and belay, or I'll shatter your hull! To larboard and starboard with lubbers!"

"That's it! That's it!" beamed the pirate, slapping his knee. "I remember now, and won't that bring them into the wind, though? Hah! Now let's think up something real stiff for Ato to try on his subjects. Come on, King, we're going to practice!"

"Stop!" coughed the Read Bird, holding up his claw.

"Stop what?" demanded Peter indignantly.

"Practicing!" sniffed Roger. "Stop practicing and be ready to act. There's something abaft our beam."

"Is it a ship?" cried Peter, dashing over to the rail. "Is it the *Sea Lion*?"

"All I see lyin' there is an island," answered

Roger in a bored voice. "Take the wheel, Master Salt, and I'll fly aloft and look her over."

"Why, here's a potato bug on my sleeve!" yelled Ato, in such excitement that he spilled half the peas. "Heigh ho! Where there's a potato bug there must be potatoes."

"Might as well say that where there's a lady bug there's bound to be a lady," observed Samuel, taking the wheel with one hand and drawing out his binoculars with the other. "Not much of a place, mates, from what I can see. Why, it's just no place at all! But we'll go ashore anyway and give Roger a rest and see whether we can pick up some potatoes and duck eggs for the cook."

"I'm going to take a sack in case there *should* be any treasure," decided Peter, as the *Crescent Moon* bore down on a long, heavily wooded slice of land.

"And I'll bring a basket in case there *should* be any potatoes," puffed Ato, hurrying off to the galley.

"And I'll take a box for specimens," said Samuel Salt, his eyes beginning to sparkle with interest and curiosity.

"Don't forget your gun. Don't forget you're a pirate," rasped Roger darkly. "Looks like a cannibal island to me and we may have a fight on our hands." Tucking *Maxims for Monarchs* under his wing to drop on Samuel's head in an emergency, the Read Bird, without waiting for his mates, flew ashore.

No castle nor dwellings of any kind were visible when the jolly-boat landed. Indeed, the island seemed utterly deserted and uninhabited. Making their way with difficulty through the tangled wood, and keeping a careful lookout for snakes and wild animals, the landing party pushed eagerly forward and finally came to a narrow footpath.

"Where there are paths there must be people," panted Ato, changing the basket from one hand to the other and trudging along determinedly. "Now I *do* hope they'll have some flour, sugar and civilized food, some butter, eggs and potatoes. I'm minded to try some of those recipes Roger's been reading me."

"Pshaw, I don't believe this path leads anywhere," complained Peter after they had followed its windings for nearly an hour. "We're just getting nowhere at all."

"Right!" called the pirate, who was a little ahead of the others. "Look here, my lad." Hurrying forward, Peter saw a crooked sign nailed so low on the trunk of a tree that he had to bend almost double to read it.

THIS PATH LEADS NOWHERE,

stated the sign defiantly.

"In that case we might as well go straight back to the boat," groaned Roger, settling in the branches of a tree. "Who wants to go Nowhere?"

"But somebody must have put up this sign," reasoned Samuel Salt, thoughtfully clipping off the tops of some weeds with his scimitar. "Let's go on. It's not far to the other side of the island and we may pick up some wild fruit or game." Deciding that this was the only sensible procedure, the four started on and in less than ten minutes had come not only to the end of the path that led Nowhere but to Nowhere itself.

"Well, shiver my liver!" blustered Samuel, pushing back his red headkerchief. "Here we are!"

"So!" sniffed Roger, elevating his bill scornfully. "So this is Nowhere, is it? Well, I've often wondered where it was and now I know. Nowhere! Huh!" With a tired flop Roger settled on Ato's shoulder and one could not blame the Read Bird for his lack of enthusiasm. Nowhere was but a grim, barren clearing in the woods. A long, low, roughly thatched cottage stood in the middle of Nowhere and from a short flag pole fluttered a brown banner emblazoned with three words:

Nowhere at all.

"Well, surely nobody lives here," gasped Peter.

"Right again!" Striding over to the cottage, Samuel Salt squinted down at the sign over the cottage door. Then, straightening up, he slapped his knee with amusement and surprise. "This says, 'Nobodies' Home,' " confided the pirate, with a broad grin. "So, mates, as nobody's home, we might as well go in and take a look around." But just as Samuel, followed by the others, started to enter the cottage, the door opened and Nobody came out. "Shiver my liver!" gulped Samuel, catching hold of Ato for support. "Shiver my liver and shatter my shins!"

"Well, you needn't shatter mine," winced the King, giving the pirate a push. "Get off my foot, Sammy, I may want to use it. What do you say we all turn around and run for it?"

"Golly!" breathed Peter. "He really has no body, Ato, just a head, some legs, and some arms."

And Peter was right, for Nobody had no body at all. For a long moment the pirates stared curiously at Nobody and Nobody as curiously stared back. Then Peter, growing uncomfortable at the absolute silence, ventured a remark.

"Nice day?" observed Peter, shuffling his feet uneasily.

"HE REALLY HAS NO BODY"

123

"No!" snapped Nobody, scowling up at Peter disagreeably. "No!"

"May we come inside and rest awhile?" inquired Ato, setting down his basket and smiling kindly at the little fellow on the doorstep.

"No!" answered Nobody, shaking his ugly head firmly. "No room."

"Ho, this fellow has the Noes," giggled Roger, ruffling up his feathers. "Do you live here all alone, Mr. Nobody?"

"Nobody Much," corrected the little man pompously, and as he spoke three more Nobodies joined him on the step.

"Nobody Else, Nobody At All and Nobody Knows!" announced Nobody Much, waving at his squat companions. "And just Nobodies," he added carelessly as dozens more of the odd little beings poured out of the cottage.

"I'd like to take one home for a specimen," whispered Samuel Salt to Peter, "but I expect it wouldn't be right. Have you anything to eat for hungry seamen, boys?" boomed Samuel, grinning broadly at the Nobodies.

"No!" yelled the Nobodies all together. "No! No! No!"

"Don't you ever eat anything yourselves?" asked Ato wonderingly.

"No!" shouted the Nobodies, even more firmly than before.

"No body, no stomach, no appetite, no use," explained Nobody Much, who seemed to be the leader of the Nobody band.

"Well, well, and well! Fancy that, Roger. The poor things never eat. Think of what they miss!" And recalling the grand dinners he had eaten in his thousand years—and the King enjoyed a good dinner as much as a good yarn—Ato shook his head pityingly. But Peter was growing more impatient and angry every minute.

"If you have nothing to eat, can you tell us the way to some place where we *can* find something?" demanded Peter in an exasperated voice.

"No way! No place! No time!" answered Nobody Much, folding his arms indifferently.

"No! No! Can't you fellows say anything but 'No'?" screeched Roger irritably.

"No!" screamed the Nobodies insolently, at which the Read Bird lost his temper and even Samuel Salt looked mad.

"Are you going to stand here and listen to these Nobodies saying nothing?" fumed Roger, jumping up and down on Ato's shoulder. "This is no kind of talk for a King. Are you a King or are you not?" Opening *Maxims for Monarchs*, Roger angrily flipped over the pages till he came to the N's, then ran his claw quickly down the leaf.

"Well, what does it say?" wheezed Ato uneasily.

"It says Nobody can say 'No' to the King," grumbled Roger, after a short silence.

"There you are!" Picking up his basket, Ato looked resignedly at the Royal Reader. "There you are, and what can we do about it? Nobody *can* say 'No' to the King."

"Well, they've certainly said it," muttered Peter. "If they weren't so little I'd jump all over them. Go on, get out of here!" exploded the boy, angrily stamping his foot. "Shoo! Scat! Get along with you! Do you hear?"

"Are you sure there's nothing to eat on the island?" bawled Samuel, as the Nobodies scampered pell mell back into their cottage.

"No! No! No!" screamed the little imps, jumping up and down and making fearful faces at the pirates. "No! No! No!" Even after the door slammed shut they could still be heard shouting.

"No! No! No!" mimicked Roger, slamming his book crossly. "They don't know what they're talking about! Back to the boat, mates. I've had enough of this place."

"But there's nothing to eat on the boat," explained Ato plaintively. "I, for one, am not going back till I find something to eat."

"Me, neither," declared Peter, forgetting all about his grammar. "Come on, fellows, let's see what's on the other side of Nowhere." So, with the Read Bird flying ahead, the three shipmates tramped morosely across the clearing and plunged into the heavy woodland on the other side of Nowhere.

CHAPTER 12

The Other Side of Nowhere

THE woods on the other side of Nowhere were not so dense and the pirates soon came out on a long stretch of sand and dunes.

"Humph!" grunted Samuel Salt, squinting off  at the sparkling blue sea. "The Nobodies were right. There's nothing on the island but gulls. Let's follow the coast till we come to the ship and maybe we can pick up some clams or beach plums." Peter winked at Ato and the King winked back, for they both knew Samuel was more liable to pick up shells and seaweed then clams, but saying nothing they proceeded amiably along the shore. Roger, flying ahead on a quest of his own, found a clump of wild berry bushes and filled first himself and then Ato's basket with the bright blue fruit. Peter came upon a wild duck's nest in the long grass behind a dune and carefully transferred the eggs to his pocket. But it was Ato who made the most astounding and valuable contribution to the larder. Quite a distance behind the others he was trudging patiently through the heavy sand when he heard a plaintive cry behind him.

"Bah! Ba-aah! Bah!" bleated a deeply nasal voice. "Bah nah nah!"

"What can that be?" pondered the King, and as the cry came again even more pleadingly, he picked his way through some heavy bushes and saw, caught between two tub trees, a fat and uncommonly handsome goat. The animal rolled its eyes sorrowfully at the King and make an unsuccessful attempt to squeeze through.

"Wait," wheezed the kind-hearted monarch sympathetically. "Wait, I'll help you." Getting behind the goat he gave such a shove that it shot forward and they both tumbled down together.

"BAH!" grumbled the King, picking himself up hurriedly. "Now I hope you're satisfied."

"Bah nah nah?" bleated the goat questioningly, and coming over, rubbed her nose sociably against the King's knee.

"Why do you keep bleating 'Bah nah nah'?" fumed Ato crossly, for he had skinned both knees and the end of his nose. At this the goat lowered her head and thinking she meant to butt him the King jumped back. But as she continued to stare at him patiently and pleasantly he gave a start of surprise.

"Great aunts and grasshoppers!" exclaimed the Cook of the *Crescent Moon*, clapping his hand to his heart. "It's a bananny goat! Wait till Peter sees this!"

"Bah nah nah?" inquired the animal, with a hopeful little skip. "Have a banana, kind sir." Lowering her head, the goat thrust her horns into the King's hands. Each horn was a fine yellow banana and as she straightened up they broke off and two more began to grow.

"Breakfast for all hands!" panted the King, staring at the bananny goat in fascination. "Bananas and cream every morning. Come with me,

goat. You're going on a voyage." The goat seemed pleased enough with the idea and kicking up her heels in a gay and carefree manner trotted cheerfully after the King. The others were already in the jolly-boat when Ato caught up with them.

"What's that?" grunted Samuel Salt, leaning heavily on his oar as Ato, followed by the goat, came splashing toward them.

"Cream for our coffee, if we had any coffee," explained the King, and calmly seizing the goat under the middle dumped her into the boat and climbed in himself. As Peter and Samuel and the Read Bird had never seen a bananny goat in their lives, it took some time for the excitement caused by her arrival to die down and for the jolly-boat to get under way.

"I'm going to call her Breakfast," announced the King, proudly patting the fat sides of his new pet. The goat, after offering each a banana, placidly went to sleep leaning against Ato's knee.

"Bananas and cream! What a breakfast for pirates!" scoffed the Read Bird, who was a bit jealous of this new shipmate.

"I can milk her," offered Peter eagerly. There had been a goat on his uncle's farm and he knew something about the creatures, not, of course, about bananny goats but enough for a fair beginning, anyway. "Gee!" he continued happily. "With duck eggs, berries and bananas and cream we'll have quite a feast, won't we? What did you find, Samuel?"

"The finest example of a pygobranchial you

131

ever saw in your whole life," boasted the pirate, tapping his specimen box proudly, "and a pulmonata that would raise your hair."

"Well, just keep the lid down," shuddered Ato, edging away. "Whatever they are I don't believe in 'em." By the time Samuel had explained his strange treasures, or endeavored to explain them, they had come to the *Crescent Moon.* Getting the goat aboard was quite a problem and after three or four vain attempts to coax her up the ladder, they made a harness of rope and pulled her to the deck. There she trotted about contentedly, bleating with interest and curiosity while Peter, Ato and the pirates hoisted the sails and Roger wound up the Anchor. Now Samuel took the wheel, the Read Bird flew off to attend to the masthead lights and Ato and Peter went below to prepare dinner, for it was already growing dark and the trip ashore had given them tremendous appetites.

"Boiled duck eggs and peas, fresh berries, bananas and cream! Not bad," announced Ato, looking critically at his well-heaped tray. "Not bad at all, but what can I get for the goat?" he queried, regarding Breakfast, who was nibbling experimentally at one of the life preservers.

"Just banana skins," called Breakfast, shaking her head so hard that both horns fell off. "Just banana skins, old fellow."

"Well, that's lucky," chuckled Peter, giving Ato a nudge. "At that rate she'll be a cinch to take care of. Look at those horns grow, will you?"

"Horns of plenty," smiled the King, waddling off toward the cabin with the tray. "Horns of plenty." After dinner Peter tied up the goat in the forecastle.

"You might slip overboard," he explained apologetically, as he slipped the rope around her neck.

"Oh, that's all right," yawned Breakfast, settling herself cozily in one of the pirates' berths.. "See you in the morning, sonny."

"Okay!" laughed Peter, picking up his lantern. "See you in the morning, madam." But, as it happened, Peter did not see Breakfast in the morning, and neither did anyone else! The forecastle—indeed, the whole bow of the ship— was buried under the mountain of bananas Breakfast had shed in the night. They rolled and slid about the lower deck, blocked every porthole and door and choked up every passageway so that the *Crescent Moon*, weighed down under the unaccustomed load, dipped far below the water line.

"Bah nah nah!" wailed the plaintive voice of the goat from the bottom of the heap. Peter and Ato, who had just come on deck, stared at one another in dismay, but the Read Bird, bidding Ato take his place at the wheel, flew screaming off to wake the pirate.

"Wake up! Wake up!" shrilled Roger, beating

133

his wings in Samuel's face. "Wake up, before that precious goat sinks the boat!" Samuel, who had been on the last long watch, rolled sleepily out of his berth at Roger's loud outcries, and dragging on his coat ran up the companionway.

"Well, shiver my liver!" raged the pirate, as the mountain of bananas, shifting backward and forward with the motion of the ship, caught his eye. "Shiver my liver and shatter my bones! Is the *Crescent Moon* a common freighter, a scow or a banana boat?" he bawled angrily. "Fall to, mates! Heave them to the fishes, and lively, too!" While Roger held the ship to her course, the others fell upon the bananas and hurled, shoved and pushed them into the sea. And for the first and last time on the voyage, Peter saw the pirate really aroused.

"It's because he loves his boat," chuckled the boy, watching out of the corner of his eye as Samuel feverishly flung bananas in twos, threes and dozens over the rail.

"When I come to that goat, I'll bust her binnacle!" exploded the pirate vindictively. "Not only her binnacle but her hatches as well."

"You can't do that, Sammy," observed Ato, stopping short with his arms full of bananas. "She's a good goat. Besides, I don't believe Breakfast has a binnacle. And she can't help growing bananas. That's her business. And bananas are a good thing to have on a voyage."

"Yes, but this is too much of a good thing," shouted Samuel, very red in the face. "Bah nah nah!" Angrily he imitated the voice of Breakfast, growing louder as the bananas grew lower. "I never want to see another banana as long as I live."

"She should walk the plank for this," said Roger unfeelingly. "She's a dangerous character and tried to sink us while we slept."

"Oh, nonsense!" mumbled Ato. "You don't know a good goat when you see one. Come on out, you poor creature, you, and get a breath of air." At last all the bananas were overboard and Ato led Breakfast, trembling and bleating, up on the deck. Peter watched rather anxiously, for he feared that Samuel in his present mood might really shove the goat into the sea, but the pirate, after one ferocious glare in the goat's direction, strode back to the cabin.

"I've thought of something," confided Ato to Peter, and sure enough he had, for when Peter got back with the milking pail, the King had tied

135

"Nobody appreciates me," blubbered Breakfast

the goat to a porthole with her head out over the water.

"Nobody appreciates me," blubbered Breakfast, shedding alternate tears and bananas into the sea. "Nobody appreciates me! I was never so humiliated in my life."

"Don't you care," said Peter soothingly. "We'll put you off on the first island we come to, and think what fun you'll have telling about your sea voyage. I'll bet you're the only goat out of the world who ever shipped on a pirate vessel."

"I'm the only bananny goat in existence," quavered Breakfast, rolling her eyes around at the boy. "And if I'd known this was a pirate ship I'd never have come a foot of the way. Are you a pirate, too, my poor misguided child?"

"Yep, I'm a pirate, too," Peter told her recklessly. "A pirate who's fond of goats," he whispered consolingly, as Breakfast gave a nervous jump. "So buck up your spirits, old lady, and all will yet be well."

"Well? Well? I feel very far from well," bleated Breakfast, resting her chin on the porthole and closing her eyes. She looked so comical that Peter had all he could do to keep from laughing. Giving her a pat he took the pail of milk and ran off to help Ato in the galley, leaving the bananny goat to reflect on the strange manners of boats and men. A high sea was running and the *Crescent Moon* pitched and rolled in a way that made Breakfast long for her native land, or any land for that matter.

A look in his specimen box had completely restored Samuel Salt to his usual good humor and he grew almost cheerful as he and Peter and Ato finished off the duck eggs and berries. No one seemed to want a banana. But now that there was no longer any danger that Breakfast would swamp the boat, the pirate felt more kindly toward the unfortunate creature and he and Ato even tried to make plans for her future. Before anything had been decided, however, and right in the middle of a lively discussion, a loud hail came from the Read Bird.

"Ship ahoy!" shouted Roger, in a regular fog horn voice. "Ship ahoy! All hands on deck and stand by for trouble!"

"Oh, golly! I'll bet it *is* the *Sea Lion* this time," cried Peter, bounding up the steps two at a time.

"Maybe it's the *Octopus*," puffed Ato, grabbing a water bottle by the neck. "Rough, bluff and relentless, now, mates. To larboard and starboard with lubbers!"

"Now, now, not too quick with that stuff," cautioned Samuel Salt, seizing the cook's shirt tail. Breathless the three arrived on deck. Roger had done well to call them. Bearing down upon them was a great, strange ship three times the size of the *Crescent Moon* with tall turrets instead of masts—such a ship as none of them had ever seen or dreamed of.

"She's running us down," gasped Peter wildly, and without waiting for orders the boy dashed for one of the port guns, which were all primed and set 'for firing, and pulling the cord sent a convincing and warning cannon ball across the enemy's bow.

"Stop! Stop! Do you want to hurt somebody?" yelled the pirate, grabbing Peter around the waist. Peter, still trembling from the shock and roar of the gun, nodded vigorously.

"Did you want 'em to sink us?" he demanded indignantly.

"Three cheers and a sofa pillow!" squalled the Read Bird, flapping his wings in wild excitement. "She's surrendered, boys. There goes the white flag. Peter has captured her. What a prize! What a prize!"

"What a surprise!" mumbled Samuel Salt uneasily. "Now we'll have to board her and all that. Give me the wheel, Roger."

"Bah nah nah!" bleated Breakfast, who had heard the shot and was trembling in every leg. "Bah nah nah!"

"Not bananas, old girl," exulted the King, snatching off his apron and tightening his hold on the water bottle. "Not bananas, but milk, flour, eggs, potatoes and butter. I'd do anything for a civilized meal, mates. *Come on!*" Brandishing his water bottle, with his whiskers bristling dangerously, Ato looked as bad an old pirate as you could ever imagine, and Peter, with his scimitar in one hand and a blunderbuss in the other, looked as determined and dangerous a young one.

CHAPTER 13
The Castle Boat

NOW, whatever might be said of Samuel Salt as a pirate, no one could question his skill as a navigator, and Peter with a little thrill of pride watched him bring the *Crescent Moon* alongside the enemy craft. His knees shook a little as the two boats swung together.

"Once a boat surrenders there's no fighting," Peter told himself confidently. "But on the other hand, suppose it is a trick to bring them closer. Ginger! What a funny boat."

"It's a floating castle,"

The Castle Boat

breathed Ato, in a hushed voice, and that more
nearly described it than anything I could tell
you. A goodly sized gray stone castle with turrets, towers and battlements rose from the deck.
A high stone wall ran round the castle and Peter's
shot had torn a gaping hole in one side of it.
The deck itself was sodded and covered with
grass, trees, arbors and flower beds. In truth it
was a veritable garden. As the pirates in some
puzzlement stared upward, a drawbridge rattled
down from the stately entrance and rested on
the top rail of the *Crescent Moon.*

"Well, lad, why don't you go aboard? She's
your prize. You did all the conquering. Go on
over and take charge." Samuel Salt gave Peter
a little push and squinted uneasily up at the
strange stately castle boat.

"Not alone!" gasped Peter, beginning to feel
rather faint and frightened. "Supposing they start
something?"

"Take the bananny goat," chuckled Roger,
from his perch on Ato's shoulder. "She'll sink
any ship if you just give her time."

"I'm going with you," declared the King stur-
dily. "I'll bet there's potatoes aboard that craft,
potatoes, meat and pie. I'm hungry, hungry
enough to fight for 'em! Come on, mates! The
white flag's still flying from the mizzen tower!"
Climbing with surprising dexterity over the rail,
Ato started over the drawbridge closely followed
by Peter and Samuel Salt, who really had no
intention of staying behind. As they tramped

141

HE SURVEYED THE PIRATES WITH BORED ANNOYANCE

resolutely and grimly forward, a tall, elegantly attired personage wearing a ducal crown appeared in the castle doorway. He surveyed the pirates with bored annoyance through his monocle and impatiently motioned for them to hurry.

"Now then, my fine fellow," thought Peter grimly, "just make one pass at us and it will be the worse for you." But the nobleman had, it seemed, no intention of resisting his captors.

"I," he announced grandly, as the pirates, a little out of breath, came abreast of him, "I am Godorkas, Duke of Dork, and this is my private castle boat. You will find the jewels and gold in the morning room on the right. Take what you wish and be quick about it, and quiet, too. This shooting gives me a headache and any confusion upsets my digestion. You have left the rest of your mates on your boat, I take it?"

"A hundred of 'em, Duke," shouted the Read Bird, as Samuel opened his mouth to say there were no other men aboard the *Crescent Moon.* "And show us the way to the pantry, fellow, to the kitchens, the larder and store rooms. *We crave food!*"

"Bhookus, show these—ah—gentlemen to the kitchen," directed the Duke, turning to a frightened looking dignitary at his side, "and kindly notify me when they have left and *what.*" Casting a withering glance at Roger, Godorkas strode swiftly into a small anteroom and slammed the door.

"Ha, ha, ha!" roared the Read Bird. "This is

grand. Lead on, Bhookus, and do what the Du-kas commands or I'll peck off your ear."

"This doesn't seem right," sighed Samuel Salt, striding reluctantly after their guide, who was fleeing like a frightened rabbit along the passage.

"We need potatoes and you know it!" puffed Ato belligerently. "Don't be a goozlebug, Sammy. Why, they're lucky to get off with their lives. Mmm—mm—hurry! I smell roast beef." The servants and retainers of the Duke had locked themselves in the upper rooms of the boat and they peered down with pale scared faces as the pirates entered the castle.

Peter, not as interested in food as Ato, turned off to the right and now stood in the center of the vast and gorgeously appointed morning room of the Duke of Dork. It was as richly and regally furnished as some of the throne rooms Peter had seen in the palaces of Oz, and true to his word, Godorkas had heaped all the jewels and gold on a pearl topped table.

"I don't believe I'll take any of these," decided Peter, who, when it came right down to sword points, was almost as poor a pirate as Samuel. "We have plenty of pearls and the old boy may need these himself." So Peter merely tiptoed around the lower rooms of the castle looking with great interest and curiosity at the treasures of its owner. The castle boat was in no way like a ship except that its tables and chairs and other furniture were fastened to the floor to keep them steady in rough weather. Peter, noting the lack of sails and rigging, funnels or engines, decided it must run by some new and electric process. He had about decided to join the others in the kitchen when a curious red cupboard caught his eye. Something alive was certainly inside and it was banging and pushing aginst the doors so hard that they creaked and bulged and threatened to burst open at any moment. Undecided, Peter stared at the cabinet and then, his curiosity getting the better of his caution, he turned the key in the door and quickly jumped backward. But not quickly enough, for out with a

furious squeal shot a plump pink pig, knocking Peter head over heels. Then, flying up on a table, it regarded him with bland interest and curiosity.

"It has wings!" gulped Peter, sitting up and rubbing the back of his head. "Wings!"

"Of course I have wings," answered the pig tartly, and spreading them wide it sailed gracefully down to the floor. "You don't look much like a pirate," observed the pig conversationally.

"Well, you don't look much like a pig," stated Peter argumentatively. "Why, I never heard of a flying pig. I've read about Pegasus, but he was a flying horse. Whoever could catch and ride him was a poet."

"Same here," grunted the pig, waddling sociably over to Peter. "Whoever rides *me* is a poet and my name is Pigasus. Good gracious, did you never hear of me? Well, get aboard Master Pirate, and see what happens. I'm rather glad you captured me. This Duke is an old bore and has never ridden me yet, though he's fond of me, I dare say, for he shut me up in that cupboard so you pirates wouldn't get me. I was a present from the Red Jinn," he grunted self-consciously.

"I've heard of him," admitted Peter, with an interested sniff. Now here, he decided, was something worth taking, and throwing his leg across the pig's broad back and holding fast to its jewelled collar he calmly waited for developments. With a pleased snort Pigasus soared through an open window and flew so swiftly round and round the castle boat that Peter was soon almost too dizzy to see.

"Stop! Stop it! Do you hear me? Whoa!
Or go some place I want to go!"

gasped Peter, much to his own surprise and the pig's amusement. He had merely meant to say "Stop," but found it impossible to speak without making verses.

> "Stop or I'll clop thee on the spine.
> Haste to the castle kitchen, swine,"

cried Peter in the next breath, and all the Duke's retainers, popping their heads out of the upper windows, shouted and roared with merriment.

"Well, why didn't you say kitchen in the first place?" chuckled Pigasus, looking mischievously back at Peter. "Here goes!" Swooping in through a window and bumping Peter's head severely as he did so, Pigasus coasted cleverly down to the floor and Peter, full of embarrassment and indignation, rolled off. Ato and Roger, briskly filling baskets and hampers with toothsome supplies from the Duke's pantry, looked up in astonishment.

"Where have you been, and what's this?" demanded the King, staring in some alarm at the pig, who was still flapping his wings and snorting gently.

"You don't mean to tell me you've been riding that pig?" shrieked Roger, dropping a can of baking powder. "What right has a low beast like that to wings, and what's it doing on a boat?"

"He'll make splendid sandwiches," murmured Ato, tapping the pig's pink sides approvingly, "and go well with the eggs. Ham on the wing; well, well and well!"

"Oh, no, he's not that kind of pig," explained Peter hastily, for Pigasus looked so startled and hurt at the King's speech that the boy felt positively sorry for him. "I'm the only egg he'll go with," he went on cheerfully. "He's a poetry pig, Ato. Gosh, all you have to do is ride on his back and you can talk in verse."

"I don't believe it," said Roger, blinking his round eyes stubbornly.

"All right, try it yourself," invited the boy, winking merrily at Pigasus. And Roger, who was really consumed with curiosity flopped down on the pig's back.

"I'm conceited and quite awful,
Speaking jawful after jawful
Of nonsense no one cares to hear.
Hard on the eye, worse on the ear,"

148

chattered Roger and promptly flew off the pig's back with a furious screech of anger while Ato and Peter fairly rocked with merriment.

"Why, he's better than a story book," puffed the King, delightedly leaning down to pat Pigasus. "I take back what I said about the sandwiches."

"Oh, that's quite all right," wheezed the pig goodnaturedly. "First you'd have to catch me, you know. Besides, I belong to this young pirate." And Pigasus leaned affectionately against Peter, who could not help feeling rather proud at such devotion.

"Maybe you'll help us move these supplies over to the *Crescent Moon*," suggested the King, with an appreciative glance at the pig's strong wings. "We've taken enough to last us the balance of the voyage, Pete. Butter, eggs, sugar, flour, canned stuff, meat, fruit, vegetables— everything!" Ato beamed, wiping his face on his sleeve. "But we'd better move on before this Duke finds there are only four of us. Where's Sammy?"

"I don't know," acknowledged Peter, climbing back on Pigasus, for he wanted to try making verses again.

"Hand up the beans, the prunes, the pie!
For we, like time, can fly, can fly!"

he found himself announcing.

"Ho, ho!" applauded Ato, handing Peter two

baskets and a box. "I could listen to you all day, but go along for time presses."

"Along we go to the *Crescent Moon*,
To return again, anon and soon,"

chortled the boy and off whisked the flying pig followed by the Read Bird, who had a basket in each claw, and by Ato and Bhookas bent double under heavy hampers. In two trips they had carried the stuff to the galley of the pirate ship, still leaving the Duke a goodly supply for himself. Now rather anxiously they began to look around for the pirate. Roger still sulkily avoided Peter and Pigasus, but Ato was in the best of humor.

"Whatever's keeping Sammy?" muttered the King, as they crossed the drawbridge for the last time. "I wish he'd hurry. I want to try my hand at a custard and a meat pie."

"I'll find him," offered Peter, and hopping back on Pigasus he flew in the window of the room to which the Duke of Dork had retired, for Peter suspected the owner of the castle boat of some treachery. What he saw was surprising enough. The pirate and the Duke sat in earnest conversation at a little table, a box of oddly shaped stones and sea shells between them. In a corner of the room, Breakfast nibbled daintily at a box of breakfast food and her half of the apartment was rapidly filling with bananas.

"Well?" inquired Peter, tumbling quickly off the pig's back.

"Well?" observed the Duke, looking up dreamily. "Captain Salt and I have spent a most enjoyable morning. It seems he is an authority on conchology and in a small way I, too, am a collector of shells."

"Bah—hh" bleated Breakfast, casting startled eyes at the winged pig, who was in his way as curious as she was in hers.

"And the Duke here is uncommonly fond of bananas, which he finds it difficult to procure at sea, so I've given him our goat to pay for the things Ato has taken," explained Samuel with an apologetic wave at Breakfast.

"How do you do, Duke?" grunted Pigasus at this point, with Godorkas, lifting his monocle, surveyed his property with some surprise.

"I see you have my pig," he murmured finally. "Well, well, take him along. He's too fat and noisy for comfort and I never did care for low verses."

"Oh, thanks! Thanks very much." Forgetting he had meant to take Pigasus anyway, Peter rushed forward and shook the Duke warmly by the hand.

"I'll drop by your island some day and we'll have another talk," promised Samuel, getting reluctantly to his feet and casting a curious and anxious glance at Peter's new pet. "I've enjoyed this immensely."

"Please do!" Rising, Godorkas bowed stiffly three times. "I had no idea pirates were so agreeable."

"Neither had I," whispered Peter in the pig's ear. "Good-bye, Breakfast. Don't let her sink your boat," he added warningly, as he climbed back on his strange steed.

"She'll swamp the boat. Oh, I should think
    so!
Bananas make a vessel sink so—

easily," carrolled Peter gaily. Covering his ears
the Duke motioned for them to hurry. So,
spreading his wings joyfully Pigasus started for
the *Crescent Moon*, Samuel Salt striding close
behind muttering happily to himself about the
habits and habitat of salt water crustaceans. The
last Peter saw of the Duke he was walking rapidly up and down the grassy deck of his curious
ship. He had a banana in each hand and between
bites was calling out calm orders to his men.
And in an astonishingly short time, the drawbridge with a rattle and clank swung back in
place and the castle boat, drawing away from
the *Crescent Moon*, swept majestically out toward the skyline.

CHAPTER 14
Snow Island

"I'LL bet there's not a ship on any sea anywhere with as strange a crew as this," thought Peter drowsily. He was reclining comfortably on a pile of sacks, his hands clasped

behind his head, lazily watching Roger and Pigasus fly races around the masts. Roger had made up with the pink pig and the two were now quite friendly, but how anyone could fly after the dinner Ato had cooked for them at noon, Peter could not imagine. "Boy, that meat pie." Patting his middle tenderly, Peter rose and strolled over to talk to the pirate.

"Well, mate," smiled Samuel Salt, "that was a lucky shot you took at the castle boat. Provisioned as we now are, we can sail round indefinitely. We're well rid of that bananny goat, too, but I don't care much for your pig."

"You don't understand Pigasus," chuckled Peter tolerantly. "He's a good sort and lots of fun. You ought to ride him, Skipper, and see what you'd say."

"I'd rather know what I'm going to say before I say it," observed Samuel, blinking dubiously up at Pigasus, who had come to rest on the cross piece of the mizzen mast. "Are you going to take him back to America with you?"

"Gosh, I'd like to," sighed the boy regretfully. "But all the animals I've met in Oz and other places never want to try a new country."

"Can't blame them," yawned Samuel, who like Peter had eaten an enormous dinner and felt very drowsy. "I wouldn't trade this ship or ocean for all the treasure in Christendom. By the way, that Duke was a strange old boy, wasn't he? Loved soft living and comfort and yet he craved the sea, too, so he fixed himself up this castle boat and enjoys both at the same time. I must stop by at the Isle of Dork some day and have another talk with him."

"In my country we have yachts for people like that," announced Peter impressively. "But of course a castle boat is much sportier."

"Sportier?" mused Samuel Salt, with a puzzled frown. "Well, I don't know about that, but

155

I wonder how she handles in a wind and what makes her go."

"Search me." Stuffing his hands in his pockets, Peter leaned luxuriously back against the rail, sniffing the keen salt air and looking fondly up at the snapping white sails overhead. "I like our kind of ship better, don't you, Skipper? She's more alive."

"Shiver my liver, yes!" beamed the pirate, bringing his hand down with a thump. "And she's yours for awhile, Pete. Four bells and your go at the wheel. Keep her headed into the wind, will you, while I go and compliment the cook?" With a grin that ended in a tremendous yawn, Samuel Salt disappeared in the direction of the galley and Peter, left to himself, fell to thinking of Samuel's men and wondering what mischief the pirates were up to and how many ships they had taken.

"Man! When we run into them there'll be real fighting," prophesied Peter thoughtfully to himself. "Well, I can fire off the guns and we'll keep Samuel mad till we capture them. If the worst comes to the worst I can fly up on Pigasus and drop weights on their heads. Roger can help at that and Ato's good most anyway you take him." Peter grew so interested and enthusiastic over a possible battle with the pirates that he almost wished the *Sea Lion* would swing into view. But as we already know, the *Sea Lion* was far from the *Crescent Moon*, and not a sail showed

on the sky line. The wind, however, was growing colder and presently Peter was annoyed to
see the jagged top of an iceberg looming up ahead.
Roger and Pigasus had finally tired of flying.
Pigasus snored peacefully beside the wheel and
Roger from his high perch in the foremast called
out sleepy remarks about the wind and weather.

"Say, I didn't know there were any polar re-
gions around here," called Peter. "Is there a
North or South Pole in these waters, Roger?"

"Certainly," coughed the Read Bird, dancing
up and down on the cross piece to keep warm.
"We must be near it, too, judging from this
wind. Kachew! Br—r-r-r. It's enough to freeze
off a body's feathers. Wake up your fat friend
and send him below for the skipper. There's
another island t'luward."

"Where?" shouted Peter, for the wind had
risen to a perfect gale.

"Yonder!" squalled Roger, waving a skinny
claw toward the east. "Yonder!"

"Yonder Island." Slowly Peter repeated the
phrase to himself, for he rather liked the sound
of it. "Maybe that is the name," he reflected
thoughtfully. "Hey, wake up, Pigasus!" He gave
the pig a sharp prod with his foot. "Here's an
island and it looks good."

"To eat?" yawned the pig, opening one eye
and rolling over on his back. After several more
prods he opened the other eye and trotted sleepily off to summon the captain. Ato came with

him, and first one and then the other surveyed
the glittering expanse of land through Samuel's
binoculars.

"We've plenty to eat and plenty to read, so
why bother with the pesky place?" puffed Ato,
blowing on his fingers and wrapping his arms
up in his apron. "Let's put about, Sammy, and
let this island freeze along without us."

"But there may be a lot of interesting specimens there," muttered Samuel, shaking his head
till his gold earrings twinkled in the sunshine.
"Luff, my boy, luff! Here, give me the wheel."
Right willingly Peter let Samuel take his place,
and hopping on Pigasus clapped his hands briskly
together.

"Ho, luff and luff, boys! Luff and luff!
The wind is high and the sea is rough;
Do you find this weather cold enough?"

Peter found himself singing out to the captain
as Pigasus trotted up and down the deck to keep
from freezing.

"There's a North Pole cat," called Roger in
a hoarse voice, and Peter, jumping off the pig,
rushed to the rail to see what on earth, or rather
on the sea, Roger was talking about. Calmly
riding the crest of the iceberg, which Samuel
had just missed very skilfully, was a huge polar
bear and he looked condescendingly down at the
boy as the iceberg swept past.

"Pshaw, that's not a North Pole cat," exclaimed Peter, in a disappointed voice. "It's a bear."

"Well, that's what we call 'em," insisted Roger, coming down with a whirr and flutter. "Ugh! Let the pig take my place for awhile. I'm frozen to the last feather."

"Come below and I'll make you some good hot coffee," wheezed Ato. "I'll make us all some. If we're to land on a frozen island we'd better be prepared. Come along, Pete. There's a lot of heavy coats and caps in the fo'cas'l."

"Bring me a muffler and a couple of over-coats," grunted Pigasus gloomily, and wiggling his ears he flew up into the rigging, making such

a comical lookout that even Samuel Salt had to laugh. By the time Peter and Ato came back, the pirate had maneuvered the *Crescent Moon* alongside the sparkling island. Pigasus, very cold and blue about the snout, flew down from the mast, and he and Samuel thankfully drank the steaming mugs of coffee Ato had brought up to them. Then, donning the heavy coats and mufflers Peter had found, the whole party made ready to land. The King had wound a woolen scarf round and round the Read Bird's neck,

and with a pair of woolen mittens on his claws Roger looked funnier than a funny valentine. After vainly trying to fit his wings and legs into one of the overcoats, Pigasus wrapped himself in a blanket, and trailing it after him like a bride's train waddled sadly after his shipmates. Lowering the jolly-boat in that choppy, icy sea was no easy task but at last it was managed. With all hands aboard, Samuel Salt pulled strongly for the shore. The island was com-

PIGASUS DRANK THE STEAMING COFFEE

pletely covered with snow and Samuel brought the jolly-boat so close that it was possible to step right out on the island itself.

Ato, the first to land, took one step and disappeared. Peter, who had jumped gaily after the King, also disappeared, and Samuel Salt and Pigasus had no sooner set foot on the island than they, too, sank immediately and absolutely out of sight.

"Help! Help! Where are you?" wailed Roger, circling wildly over the four jagged holes. Touching the ground fearfully with one mitten, the Read Bird gave a frightened squawk.

"Why, it's snow!" blubbered Roger brokenheartedly. " 'S'no island at all! They're drowned, frozen and sunk forever. Oh! Oh! Oh!" Now, as Roger—indeed, as all of them, by this time— had discovered, the island was but a blanket of snow floating treacherously on top of the icy ocean. The crew of the *Crescent Moon*, plunging instantly through the top crust, had very nearly sunk to the bottom. Peter was the first to come up. Gasping and choking he floundered about, and Roger, though not nearly strong enough to pull him out, jerked him by the hair and shoulders and shed tears of relief and thankfulness on his head. Finally Peter reached the edge and managed to swim to the boat and drag himself aboard. Samuel Salt, looking more like a sea lion than a pirate emerged next and puffing and blowing through his frozen whiskers looked frantically around for the King. Pigasus, once

he rose to the surface, spread his wet wings, and squeaking with chill and displeasure flew straight back to the ship. Ato, the heaviest of all, was the last to appear. With icicles forming on his nose and beard he clawed his way through the waves desperately and swallowed nearly a barrel of the Nonestic Ocean before the pirate, Peter and Roger managed to haul him to safety.

"Well, Sammy," choked the King, sinking in a wet and exhausted heap on the bottom of the boat, "I hope you're satisfied. Choo, choo. *ka-choo*! We've doubtless picked up some fine specimens of bronchitis, pneumonia and rheumatism!" Breaking the icicle from his nose, Ato regarded the pirate as severely as his chattering teeth would permit, and Samuel, making indistinct noises that may have been sympathy or may have been salt water mixed with coughing, seized the oars and pulled vigorously for the *Crescent*

163

Moon. Roger's wings had frozen to his sides and a more miserable bird it would have been hard to discover. Without a word and more dead than alive, the explorers crawled up the ladder and made a bee-line for the galley.

Pigasus, sensible creature that he was, had set the coffee pot on the fire. Already thawed out and comfortable, he helped the pirates out of their wet and frozen garments. After changing into dry ones they gathered gratefully around the stove, consuming vast quantities of scalding coffee and biscuits left over from dinner. After the twentieth biscuit and fifth mug of coffee, Samuel Salt went up on deck and with great satisfaction the company below felt the great ship swing round and head for the south and warmer waters.

"Snow Island," scolded Roger, taking a huge bite out of his biscuit, "is snow place for pirates."

"Snow place for me; snow place for you;
It shivered my liver and tonsils, too!"

added Peter, who for the moment sat on Pigasus.

"Ha, ha! That pig's a caution," roared Ato, who was warm by this time and quite cheerful again. "If I were not so fat I'd ride him myself."

"He makes you talk nothing but nonsense," sniffed the Read Bird, fluttering his wings to see if they were completely thawed. Peter chuckled as he jumped off the pig's back.

"But such nice nonsense," he smiled, giving Pigasus such an affectionate pat that his ears waved and his little pink tail curled with pleasure and gratification.

CHAPTER 15
Mount Up

THERE was a stiff breeze blowing and the *Crescent Moon*, skimming the waves like a great white sea bird, sped swiftly toward the south, coming at evening to a strange and mysterious island. It rose like a mountain out of the sea and was so steep and craggy that Ato groaned at the mere thought of going ashore.

"Let's not notice it," shuddered the ship's cook, averting his eyes from the forbidding mass of rock and sandstone. "Let's anchor here for the night and sail by in the morning. We

should be headed for Ev, anyway, if we ever intend to catch up with my ship, and I don't believe we'll ever find yours, Samuel."

"I'm afraid you're right," agreed the pirate gloomily. "That lubber, Binx has probably run the *Sea Lion* aground by this time."

"Well, what will you do if you never find them?" inquired Peter, who liked to get things settled.

"Oh, I'll just cruise around and do a little exploring," said Samuel. "Couldn't wish for pleasanter sailing than we've had this voyage. How about you fellows cruising with me?" he proposed hopefully.

"I'll stay if we don't find the *Octopus*," promised Ato promptly. "I like the life and I'm growing fonder of cooking than kinging."

"If Ato stays, I'll stay, too," chirped Roger, looking affectionately at his master. "He needs somebody to look after him and read out the recipes."

"If Peter stays, I'll stay," grunted Pigasus, resting his chin on Peter's knee.

"Boy! I'd like to," exclaimed Peter, rubbing the pig's ears thoughtfully. "But my grandfather must be worried about me, and pretty soon I'll have to be getting back to the team. We've some stiff games on this month. I'll hate to leave this ship, but I guess we had better start for Ev, Skipper. Then I'll travel on to the Emerald City and ask Ozma to send me back to Philadelphia."

"And what about me?" inquired Pigasus in an injured voice.

"Oh, you can stay in the Emerald City with Ozma," Peter assured him hastily. "You are so interesting and clever she'll be glad to have you 'round."

"He's round all right," muttered Roger. "A pig in a palace. Ho! They'll put ribbons in your ears and make you wear a bib, Pinky, dear."

"Don't listen to him, he's only teasing," whispered Peter, putting his arm around Pigasus. "You'll like it awfully."

"Well, then, it's all settled!" With a regretful sigh the pirate looked at Peter. "In the morning we sail for Ev." But in the morning there was not even the vestige of a breeze, and the *Crescent Moon*, idle and motionless, rested in the shadow of the great sea mountain and all day her crew waited impatiently for her sails to lift or stir. But the wind had died down utterly.

"We may be here for months," prophesied the pirate, who was taking this opportunity to sort and label his various specimens. "Once, off the Jalacasco Islands, I was becalmed a year and seven days."

"A year!" cried Peter, in genuine consternation and dismay. "Golly, can't we do something about it? Why, if I stay away a year my grandfather will think I'm dead and the fellows will make Billy Hastings captain of the team." Samuel shook his head soberly and Peter, feeling extremely annoyed and uneasy, paced up and down the deck. Next day was as calm as the one before and each hour Peter grew more impatient and restless. A month or even a year seemed a small matter to Samuel Salt and to Ato. Dwelling as they did in a magic country they would live on for centuries, but to Peter such a delay seemed a positive calamity.

"Mind if I go ashore?" he asked, soon after the noon meal on the second day. "It will help pass the time and maybe something will turn up while I'm gone."

"I'll carry you over," offered Pigasus obligingly, as Samuel looked doubtfully at Ato.

"And I'll go along to see that nothing happens," volunteered Roger, who wanted to stretch his wings. "And I'll fly back for help if any is needed."

"Well, in that case I see no harm in it," murmured the King, from where he was sitting on a pickle keg beating up a cake batter. "But it would be silly for Sammy and me to climb that mountain, and the pig can't carry us all."

"You bet I can't!" snorted Pigasus, flapping his ears vigorously. "Hop up, Peter, and mind you keep a hot supper for us, Cooky, dear. Flying gives me a dreadful appetite."

> "So long fellow pirates and shipmates, goodbye!
> No mountain's a mountain to folks who can fly,"

169

"Up Mount Up let us fly!"

called Peter, as Pigasus rose like an animated pink sausage into the air.

"Do I have to listen to that stuff all afternoon?" grunted Roger who had no difficulty in keeping up with the flying pig. Peter grinned, for it was fun to have your thoughts put in verse, especially when you never knew just how they would turn out.

> "Let's start at the bottom and fly to the top,
> And when we see something we want to
> see, stop,"

suggested Peter next.

"Yes, that is a clever idear, dear," hummed the pink pig, glancing mischievously back at Peter.

> "Don't you dare call me dear,
> or I'll box your pink ear,"

retorted Peter sharply, as the Read Bird burst into a series of hilarious screeches. By this time they had come to the foot of the mountain. A large flag fluttered from a pole set among the rocks.

MOUNT UP

announced the flag in crimson letters.

"Mount Up?" read Roger, squinting hard at the red letters. "Well, I'm a bow-legged sailor!"

"I'm glad we don't have to mount up Mount Up," panted the pink pig, his tongue hanging

171

out from the exertion of flying. "I'd rather float
up."

"So would I, so would I;
Up Mount Up let us fly!"

urged Peter, who was curious to know whether
anyone lived on the wild and desolate heights of
the sea mountain. So Pigasus, keeping close to
the rocks, began to fly slowly upward. For a time
it seemed that Mount Up was uninhabited, but
as they came nearer to the summit a quaint and
curious country spread out below them. Its name,
spelled out on the mountain side in a series of
bubbling fountains, was Cascadia and its people
were entirely formed of water. Gaily they poured
themselves down over the rocks headfirst and
recklessly. Then, when they had gone down as
far as they wished, they would jet up in a sparkling fountain to the top and start cascading all
over again. As Pigasus flew lower so Peter could
see better, a ripple of mirth ran through the
crowd and bubbling over with interest and
friendliness, the Cascadians waved and shouted
at the travellers and sprayed them with a shower
of water.

"That's a wet way to spend your life," scoffed
Roger, shaking his feathers fretfully. "Falling
up and down a mountain. Huh! Not for me!"

"Oh, it wouldn't be so bad if you were made
like they are," observed the pig, flying out of
range as a group of Cascadians hurled themselves upward.

172

GAILY THEY POURED THEMSELVES DOWN

173

"What all this water fallin',
This splash and dash and spray?
Do you really like to waterfall
And cataract that way?"

inquired Peter, and then burst into a laugh at
his own verses.

"Of course! Of course!" gushed a waterman
in a moist whisper. "What could be grander than
slipping and sliding down a mountain?"

"Lots of things! Lots of things!" challenged
Roger, flapping his wings scornfully. "But we
haven't time to explain them. Won't Ato enjoy
hearing about these Cascadians?" he chuckled,
settling happily on Peter's shoulder. "And I must
remember that last verse you made, too. He'll
love that."

"Please don't forget that I am responsible for
the verses," Pigasus reminded him jealously. "Not
a stanza could he make if he were not riding on
my back. Hello! Here we are at the top. Shall I
fly over, or come down?"

"Come down, Pigasus, down and whoa!
We'll look around before we go,"

directed Peter. As the pink pig set all four feet
on the ground, Peter tumbled hastily off his
back.

"It makes you feel kinda funny spouting poetry *all* the time," he confessed in a low voice
to Roger. "Pretty good view from here, isn't it?"

174

"I've seen worse," conceded Roger, perching on a boulder. "Our ship looks like a toy boat."

"Here's an eagle's nest," exclaimed Peter, and sure enough, resting on three crooked stones there was an eagle's nest with one egg in it. Picking up the egg, which was large and unusually heavy, Peter was astonished to see written on one side: DO NOT BREAK! "Why, this can't be a real eagle's egg," said Peter, carrying the egg over to the Read Bird. "Real eggs don't have writing on them. And why shouldn't I break it if I feel like it?"

"It might be a bad egg," chattered Roger nervously, "a big ba-ad egg. Better not meddle with it. Great Goosefeathers! Now see what you've done!" Without really intending to, as he let it slide from hand to hand, Peter dropped the egg on the rocks and with a tremendous bang it exploded, filling the air with smoke, fire and brimstone, for it was, as Roger had hinted, a very bad egg indeed. Not only that, but the ground beneath their feet began to rock and tremble violently.

"Run! Fly! Where's that pig?" screamed Roger, hurling himself into the air. Pigasus had already flown out of danger's way and rushing to the edge of the mountain Peter clasped his arms around a tree and closed his eyes. With a jolt that nearly uprooted the tree, the whole center of Mount Up shot into the air, and when Peter ventured to look around a monstrous head was sticking out of the hole.

"WHO BROKE THAT EGG?"

Mount Up

"Who broke that egg?" roared the owner of the head, the largest, ugliest ogre Peter had ever seen outside of a story book. For a moment he was too petrified to answer. Then, seeing that Pigasus was flying bravely to help him, he took courage and shouted defiantly:

"I did!"

"Well, good for you!" roared the ogre in such a loud voice that Peter was flattened against the tree trunk. "You have not only broken the egg, but the enchantment that shut me up in this mountain. Ha! In two shakes and a kick I'll be out of here and on my way home. But tell me first what I can do to repay you." Peter's hair stood on end at the mere thought of the giant kicking his way out of the mountain and he wondered sympathetically what would become of the Cascadians when he did.

"Stop! Wait!" he called breathlessly. "Don't move or you'll knock me off!"

"Well, I've waited five hundred years so what's a few minutes longer," rumbled the ogre cheerfully. "But my nose is itchy young one and pretty soon I'll have to pull out my arm and scratch it. How long must I stand here to please you?"

"Oh, just till my flying pig comes back," Peter told him, waving wildly for Pigasus, who was circling hesitantly overhead, to descend. The pig fluttered uncertainly down.

"Just who enchanted you?" called the Read Bird, who had recovered from the shock of the explosion and was listening to the conversation

177

with close attention and interest. "And what is your name, if any?"

"Og!" roared the giant, putting back his head so he could get a better view of the Read Bird. "I, you must know, am the Ogre of Ogowon. The witch who lives on the next island objected to my snoring so she cast a spell that shut me up in this mountain."

"Dear, dear!" murmured Roger, resting his bill in his claw.

"If you call it 'dear, dear' to be shut up in a mountain for five hundred years, you're a fool!" shouted the ogre, so ferociously that Roger spread his wings and made a wild swoop for the *Crescent Moon*.

"Climb up! Climb up, Peter, before he smashes us both!" begged Pigasus, his fat sides quivering like jelly. "Oh, why did we ever come here?"

"Wait," whispered the boy. "I have an idea, Pigasus. He said he wanted to help us and I believe he can!"

"Do you really want to do something for me?" he called in a shaky voice, as the ogre continued to glare wrathfully after the Read Bird.

"Didn't I say so?" grumbled the ogre, whose temper was as ogreish as his stature.

"Well, can you blow hard?" called Peter boldly. "Our ship is becalmed at the foot of this mountain and if you give us a start for the south it would be a great help."

"Poof, that's easy," boasted the ogre, as Peter jumped on the pig's back. "I'll give you a minute to get aboard, and then, ha, ha! I'll blow you into the next ocean." With an agonized squeak, Pisasus shot into the air and fairly coasted down to the *Crescent Moon*, afraid to look back for fear the mountain would fly apart and destroy them. Dropping on the deck, Peter panted out directions and explanations, Samuel Salt and Ato pulled up the anchor and hoisted sail and then breathlessly they all waited for the ogre to keep his word.

"We'll be swamped or sunk!" groaned Roger, hiding his head under Ato's old blue shirt. "Never trust an ogre. That's *my* advice."

CHAPTER 16
The Rise of the
Crescent Moon

IT seemed at first that Roger might be right, for the fierce and furious blast that suddenly struck the ship lifted her a foot out of the water and then sent her hurling south like a balloon before a hurricane. Indeed, it took all hands to keep the *Crescent Moon* to her course, and with Peter, Ato and the pirate hanging to the wheel she bucked and plunged like a bronco that had never been ridden. Pigasus and Roger, crouching in the cabin, expected the ship to fly to pieces any minute and shouted dis-

mally to one another above the snap of her sails
and the creak of her timbers. But the *Crescent
Moon* had been stoutly built and did not go to
pieces but sped with the swiftness of a torpedo
for the coast of Ev.

"We'll be smashed!" shivered Peter, as the
cliffs and rocks of the mainland loomed ahead.

"This will knock eight bells out of us, all
right," panted the pirate, gritting his teeth grimly.
"Better be ready to jump, boys!" Ato, after one
glance at the dangerous looking coast, closed his
eyes tight and holding his fat middle tried to
think of all the pleasant stories he had ever read
or heard of. But the Ogre of Ogowon must have
been as long of sight as he was of breath, for,
on the very edge of Ev and destruction, the wind
ceased and the ship slid quietly and peacefully
into a pleasant bay.

"What a blow! What a blow!" groaned the
King, leaning weakly against the rail.

"What a blower, you mean, don't you?" sighed
Peter, sinking in a limp heap to the deck. "Whew,
what a wind! Oh-go-on—well, that's a good name
for that ogre. I thought we'd go on and on and
never stop. Come on out, boys. It's all over now!"

"Are you sure?" quavered the Read Bird,
sticking his head through a porthole. "S-say,
what's that ship? Ato! Ato! There's the *Octopus*,
or I'm a wall-eyed woodcutter!" And the *Octopus*
it certainly was, for the ogre had blown them
straight to Menankypoo.

"And there's the *Sea Lion*!" bellowed Samuel

Salt. "Look! Over there—with red sails! Shiver my liver and shatter my shins, mates, how did these rascals ever get together?"

"Now, Sammy! Now, Sammy!" Ato slapped the pirate hard between the shoulders. "Rough, bluff and relentless, remember! Shiver your timbers and all the rest of it."

"Oh," cried Peter, getting wearily to his feet. "Isn't this doggone? Do we have to fight before we even get our breath?"

"There's nobody aboard the *Octopus*," reported Roger, who had flown across to investigate, "and your ship's deserted, too, Master Salt, but everything's shipshape."

"Battle shipshape," muttered the pirate darkly. "Shiver my liver, we'll just go ashore and see what these rogues have to say for themselves. And what's all this light and shine on the water around here, anyway?" Peter had already noticed the singular glow on the waves, but as nobody could explain or account for it, they tossed over the anchor and lowered the jolly-boat.

"I'm not much of a fighter," admitted Pigasus, settling in the bottom of the boat, "but I can carry you out of danger's way if the battle goes against us, Peter."

"Yes, and you and Roger can drop rocks on the pirates and Octagon Islanders," proposed the boy, who had brought along two daggers besides his gun.

"I've some books for that, too," sniffed Roger, with a reassuring wink. Samuel Salt said noth-

The Rise of the *Crescent Moon*

ing, but from his stern expression and the way he fingered the edge of his scimitar, Peter felt that the buccaneers were due for a large surprise. Landing without difficulty they scrambled up the beach and hurried on to the city. There was not a soul in the streets and the castle, when they reached it, was quite silent and deserted.

" 'Menankypoo!' " wheezed Ato, leaning over to read the jewelled letters on the door. " 'Menankypoo. Quiet, please!' That's a funny name for a country, and it's surely quiet enough. Do you suppose our men have conquered the place, Sammy?"

"Looks that way," answered the pirate, noting the disorder and confusion everywhere in the castle. "But where have they gone and what mischief are they up to now?" As if to answer his question, faint cries and halloos came echoing up from somewhere below. Following the feeble outcries, Peter, Ato and the pirate, afoot, preceded by Roger and Pigasus, a-wing, clattered down the steps of the castle, down one flight, down another, till they came to the cellar, and still down, till they reached a damp and dismal dungeon at the very bottom. A dim light was burning, and looking through the gold bars in the dungeon door they could see two figures tied together on the floor.

"Maybe they can tell us what happened," whispered Peter. "Shall we go in? Gosh, Skipper, they look like pirates!"

"They *are* pirates," breathed Samuel Salt,

183

pressing his face against the bars. "Bless my boots and buckles if it isn't Binx and Peggo! Ship ahoy, mates! What's the trouble here?"

"Help! Help!" cried the pirates, their voices weak and hoarse from much calling. Turning the rusty key, Samuel, followed by his shipmates, strode into the dungeon. With his hands on his hips Samuel looked scornfully down at the discomfited pair.

"Ha! So this is what comes of mutiny," mused the captain of the *Crescent Moon* softly. "Got youselves caught and captured and trussed up

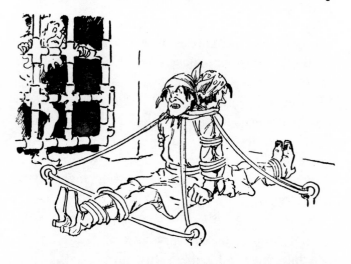

like fowls on market day. So this is your idea of pirating. Who planned all this? Who's captain and where's the rest of the crew?" The pirates winced at every word of their former leader.

"They've gone to conquer Oz," explained Binx in a weak whisper.

"To conquer Oz?" roared Samuel, bristling with surprise and displeasure. "What right have pirates to fight ashore? Who gave them that idea?

"The Gnome King," groaned Peggo, making an unsuccessful attempt to roll over. "That sneaking, thieving little rogue of a Gnome King, dim his portlights! We made him chief so he would show us the way to Oz and he promised to share all its riches and treasure, but he means to have everything himself. He's got a magic stick and a Cuckoo Clock Wizard Man. He made us march and drill and work like slaves. And now he's taken our men and those silly Octagon Islanders and gone off without us—gone and left us to starve in this dungeon like dogs."

"Did you say the Gnome King?" exclaimed Peter, dropping on his knees beside the pirates. "Why, I thought Ruggedo was dumb and could not speak."

"Dumb!" raged Peggo bitterly. "Why, he can talk faster and badder than any pirate I ever shipped with. Dumb? Why he's got enough magic to conquer this whole country and before another day he'll be Emperor of Oz. *Emperor of Oz*, that little bunch of bone and whiskers."

"So that was the chief you picked in my place," sighed Samuel Salt, shaking his head mournfully.

"And that was the King my subjects chose in mine," wheezed Ato, rolling his eyes up to the cobwebbed ceiling. "Well, well, and what do you think of it, Peter?"

185

"I think somebody had better start after them," exclaimed Peter in a husky voice. "I think somebody had better warn Ozma before they reach the Emerald City. Gosh, this is about the tenth time Ruggedo has tried to conquer Oz. Doesn't he ever learn anything? When did he start? How is he going to cross the Deadly Desert?"

"This morning," Peggo told him dolefully. "That Clock Man has some magic device for crossing the desert and they expect to be in the Emerald City about eight bells."

"*Eight Bells!*" shouted Peter, jumping to his feet in a hurry. "I'll have to start right off. How on earth shall I ever get there in time? How on earth and how ever?"

"Not on earth at all. On me," snorted Pigasus, trotting confidently forward. "I can fly that distance and we may beat them yet."

"Oh, Piggins, that's a grand idea!" And before Ato or the pirate could do anything to stop him, Peter jumped on the pig, and Pigasus, spreading his white wings, soared off like a small pink dirigible for Oz.

"It'll do no good," moaned Peggo dismally. "What can one small boy do against that villain? The standing stick will bring him to a halt and Ruggedo will capture the city in spite of him."

"Oh, why did we ever let him go?" gasped Ato, clasping and unclasping his fat hands.

"Shall I fly after them?" asked Roger, who had grown terribly fond of Peter and even felt a sort of tolerant affection for the pig.

"No! Wait! What, oh, what shall we do first?" panted Ato, seizing Samuel by the sleeve.

"Untie these ropes and we'll help you," begged Binx hoarsely.

"Shiver my liver! A fine help *you've* been!" rumbled the pirate severely. "I've a notion to leave you as you are forever."

"Not that! Not that!" The buccaneers screamed so piteously that Samuel finally relented and untied their bonds.

"Let's get back to the boat," sighed the pirate unhappily. "I can't think properly ashore. Let's get back to the boat and try to get our bearings!" As they trudged slowly and mournfully back to the *Crescent Moon*, Peggo and Binx told them all that had been happening, how they had first captured Menankypoo and tossed the inhabitants into the sea, how Ruggedo had appeared and promised to help them conquer Oz, and how his magic stick and miserable temper had made life unbearable for them and for the Octagon Islanders, who had joined them later.

"Did he take the women and children to Oz, too?" asked Ato, his eyes snapping with anger and indignation. "Where are the women and children of the Octagon Isles?"

"He shut them up in some cave or other so they would not tell his plans," explained Binx sourly. "You ought to see your Islanders now, Mr. King. A sorrier, shabbier bunch of rebels I've never set my eyes on, except perhaps my own shipmates."

"Serves 'em jolly right," scolded the Read Bird savagely. "The idea of leaving an island like ours and a King like you. It will be a good lesson for them, Ato."

"Yes, but learning it may kill them," groaned the soft-hearted sovereign. "They may be destroyed by magic. We may never see any of them again, Roger. Think of that!"

"Then we'll just ship along with Captain Salt and enjoy ourselves," said the Read Bird unfeelingly. "I'll be a sea bird and you a seacock from now on. What's the matter with that?" Ato only groaned and Samuel smiled wryly at Roger's efforts to cheer the poor King. He was too worried to join in the conversation himself and his only thought was to get aboard the *Crescent Moon* and try to think things out, calmly and collectedly. Before doing so he sent Peggo and Binx off to the *Sea Lion*, for Samuel did not yet feel kindly enough toward these two rascals to have them on his own ship. And much subdued and sobered by their experiences with the Gnome King, the pirates were glad enough to obey him. Once aboard the *Crescent Moon* Samuel rushed to the cabin, and flinging himself down on his berth tried to think of some way to stop Ruggedo before he reached the capital of Oz, and to help Peter before the Gnome King's magic destroyed him.

"If it were just a sea battle we might stand a chance," worried the pirate. "But with only a ship how are we to reach the Emerald City, and with no magic of our own how are we to fight

A SILVERY BLUE SMOKE SPIRALED UPWARD

189

magic? Shiver my bones, I'd give my head for the ogre!" Dropping his chin in his palm Samuel stared gloomily across at Peter's berth. Where was his brave little shipmate and cabin boy now? Facing what dangers and perils with no one to help him? These forlorn and dismal thoughts were suddenly halted by the sight of a dark object beside Peter's berth. Leaning over to examine it more closely Samuel saw that it was the flask Peter had fished out of the sea. The side, with its annoying label, DO NOT OPEN, was uppermost, and as Samuel bent over to pick up the bottle, the cork, loosened by the continual bumps and bangs it had suffered on the voyage, fell out. Immediately a silvery blue smoke spiraled upward, filling the cabin, curling out of the portholes and wrapping the entire ship in a misty blue veil. Throwing down the cask, convinced that some dire calamity would overtake them, Samuel dashed out on deck. The *Crescent Moon* rose up like a giant gull and, flapping he sails like wings, flew lightly over Menankypoo.

"Quick, head for the Emerald City!" squalled Roger, the first to recover. "This is what comes of calling your ship the *Crescent Moon*, Master Salt. The *Crescent Moon* has riz!" Grabbing the wheel Samuel quickly told about the mysterious flask.

"How do you know we'll stop when we come to the Emerald City?" shuddered Ato, blinking at the clouds careening dizzily by. How do you know we won't drop any minute and break to pieces?"

"We don't," croaked Roger raising his claw solemnly, "we don't know anything at all!" Hopping on Ato's shoulder he stared in giddy consternation at the countries and cities whirling beneath their bow and at the dangerous looking desert ahead. "If we drop on this desert," chattered the Read Bird, dancing up and down with nervousness, "all will indeed be over. Great goosefeathers, here we go!"

CHAPTER 17
Pigasus in Oz

WHILE all this was happening aboard the *Crescent Moon*, Peter was rushing recklessly toward Oz. For a pig, Pigasus flew uncommonly fast and before Peter had time to plan or think of a way to outwit Ruggedo, they had crossed Ev, flashed over the Deadly Desert and entered the kingdom of Oz.

"Do you see the Gnome
   King's army
Marching anywhere be-
   low?
They have to pass this way
To reach the Capital, you
   know;

Fly closer to the ground
So we can look for them. Fly low!"

called Peter, as Pigasus swept over the Yellow
Land of the Winkies.

"I see nothing of an army. But here's a silver
castle," snorted Pigasus, coasting down a little
breeze, his blue eyes twinkling with pleasure
and excitement.

"It's not a silver castle;
It's a castle built of tin;
The Emperor of the Winkies
Lives down there, when he's in.
Nick Chopper, the Tin Woodman—
You have heard of him I s'pose,
He's made of tin outside and in
And never needs new clothes,"

explained Peter aloud. "Darn these verses,"
grumbled the boy to himself. "I sound like a
nursery rhyme book." Riding Pigasus did have
its disadvantages and it was rather provoking
when Peter felt so worried and serious to keep
spouting rhymes every time he opened his mouth.
"Oh, well, it won't last much longer," thought
Peter consolingly, as the pig shot over the Tin
Woodman's palace. Peering between his white
wings strained his eyes for a glimpse of the pirates or Octagon Islanders. But without seeing
a sign of the Gnome King or his allies, they flew
over the entire Winkie Country, passing the
Scarecrow's corn-ear residence, Jack Pumpkin-

head's cozy pumpkin cottage and coming at last
to the Fairy Capital itself.

"I'm afraid they've beaten us, Peter," grunted
the pig, as they drew nearer. "What do we do
when we get inside?"

"That depends, that depends,
If we're not too late
We'll save my friends,"

answered Peter, looking anxiously down at the
familiar and lovely spires of Ozma's castle.

"I'll fly a bit higher now," decided Pigasus
warily. "Those pirates might take a pop at us."
All the round, emerald-domed little houses and
shops in the city were closed up tight, their
windows shuttered and darkened; neither was
there a person to be seen on the streets. But as
Pigasus circled above the castle they saw two
pirates glumly guarding the gates.

"Man! Ruggedo's probably got that belt and
changed everybody into cobblestones by now,"
thought Peter, his heart thumping with fright
and anxiety. "We'll just take a look and if he's
wearing the magic belt I'll fly off to Glinda for
help." Glinda, the Good Sorceress of the South,
is, as most of us know, one of Ozma's greatest
friends and most powerful allies. In a short tense
verse, Peter directed the pig to a large emerald-
studded window above the throne. Luckily this
window was open, and when Pigasus, almost
holding his breath, stuck in his head, Peter gave
a quick gasp of relief.

Ozma was still unharmed and was seated on
her great chair of state, surrounded by all the
celebrities and councillors of her court. The
window was so high that no one in the Emerald
Throne Room noticed Peter, but at his second
look the boy's heart dropped with a sickening
thud to his left shoe, for facing Ozma was Ruggedo himself! Ruggedo, fairly bristling with daggers; Ruggedo, wearing the red headgear of the
pirates and the magic belt that had caused so
many wars and revolutions in Oz. Beside him
stood the mischievous Cuckoo Clock Man, holding up the ebony stick. Ruggedo himself, with
folded arms and red eyes glittering with malice
and satisfaction, was gloating over his captives.

"At last!" rasped the Gnome King hoarsely.
"At last I have you in my power. You, you, you
and you!" With little stabs of his dagger he in-
dicated Ozma, Dorothy, the Wizard of Oz and
the Scarecrow, and throwing back his head burst
into wild, hysterical laughter. "You thought because I had lost my speech I was powerless and
helpless! Well, I'll show you. I've got back my
speech and my belt, and when I finish telling
you I'll turn you into boxes and barrels and make
a bonfire to celebrate my victory over the famous
Ozma of Oz. I, Ruggedo the Rough, will now
be ruler of Oz—of Oz and Ev forever and even
afterward. Do you hear? Do you hear?" At each
sentence he stamped his foot and his voice grew
louder, but if the celebrities heard they gave no
sign. Calmly, bravely, without a word, Ozma

and her courtiers faced complete and utter an-
nihilation.

"Why do they stand and stare like that?
Jump on him Piggins—let's knock him flat!"

burst out Peter, digging his heels into the pig's
fat sides. With a valiant squeal, Pigasus hurled
himself down toward the pirate gnome. But directly above the throne he was brought to so
sharp a stop that Peter almost shot between his
ears.

"It's the stick," panted Pigasus, trying in vain
to move his legs and wings. "I can't budge an
inch, boy! Boy, we're petrified!" The sudden and
unexpected appearance of Peter and the flying
pig threw the company into the utmost confusion. Ozma and Dorothy, the Scarecrow and Tik
Tok, recognizing the boy from Philadelphia, called
to him in frantic voices to fly out of danger's
way; for though the conjurer's stick held them
motionless, they could still speak. But it was
already too late. Pigasus could move neither
backward or forward and sputtering with wrath
and discomfort hung limply in the air. Ruggedo,
as startled as anyone at this strange interrup-
tion, blinked up in astonishment at the plump
pig and its rider. After a long, puzzled look he
gave a furious bounce.

"Prunes and pretzels!" shouted the Gnome
King. "If it isn't that meddlesome Peter from
Philadelphia. This is good, too good! Look at

him, Clocker! That's the boy who hit me with the silence stone. Ha, ha, ha! Shall I turn him into a drum and have him beaten every day, or to a door mat? What do you say, Clocker, what do you say?"

It was exactly six o'clock, and above the cries of the Oz folk and the indignant verses of Peter, the cuckoo screamed defiantly six times, and then, whizzing through the air, handed a yellow paper to Ozma and another one to Peter. Two words were written on each paper. "Snif! Snif!" Ozma read the Wise Man's message quite calmly and then held it up for the others to see. Peter tore his into fragments and while they were exclaiming indignantly over Clocker's impertinence, the cuckoo, on its way back to its master, flew right under the nose of the flying pig. With a wrathful snort Pigasus opened his mouth and in one gulp swallowed the saucy bird. The effect was alarming and unexpected. In the cuckoo rested all of the Wise Man's brains and intelligence. Deprived suddenly of all power to think, Clocker dropped the magic cane and toppled helplessly over on his nose, breaking his glass face and lying like a log at Ruggedo's feet. It all happened so abruptly that the Oz folk had scarcely time to realize they were free to move before the gnome snatched up the standing stick himself.

"Derm! Worm! Pachyderm!" stormed Ruggedo, shaking the stick at Pigasus. "You shall suffer for this!" Pigasus was suffering already, to tell the truth, for to have a wooden bird fluttering and beating its wings inside of one is upsetting and awful indeed, and while the Gnome King raged Pigasus squealed and Peter tried in vain to quiet him.

> "You tried to save us, Piggins, don't feel blue;
> Never mind, I will find some way to save you!"

"It's not my mind," groaning the pig, pink tears streaming down his cheeks, "It's my middle. It's driving me cr-crazy!"

"Cuckoo," corrected the Scarecrow, rolling his eyes solemnly up at the pig. "You *would* feel that way with a cuckoo inside of you. But you've done us a great service, nevertheless."

> "Preserve us, a service that's making him nervous,"

sputtered Peter.

"This hardly seems the time for verses," sighed Ozma, looking reproachfully at the little boy.

"He can't help it. It's m-my fault," blubbered Pigasus. "Anybody riding on my back has to make verses and be a poet."

"Silence!" roared Ruggedo, pushing Clocker to one side with his foot. "And as for you, Brother Goose," he waved his dagger menacingly at Peter, "one more verse and I'll turn you into a bookworm and tread on you."

"WHERE ARE THE TREASURES OF OZ?"

"If you intend to transform us, kindly do so," commanded Ozma, staring haughtily at the ugly little gnome. "We've heard about enough from you. You have the magic belt. Well then, *use* it!"

"That's right," agreed the Scarecrow. "I'd rather be a rock than listen to him any longer." Peter, stiff and uncomfortable as he was, could not help but admire the spirit and bravery of the Oz folk. But their courage seemed only to enrage Ruggedo the more.

"Huh!" sneered the gnome contemptuously. "I'll transform you when I'm bad and ready and not before. Tell me first where you have hidden the magic dinner bell, the magic picture and the Wizard's black bag. Do you think I'm going to waste my time looking for them?" Drawing himself up to his full height, Ruggedo glared at Ozma. "I command you to tell me where you have hidden the treasures of Oz," he shouted, his eyes bulging out like bugs.

"Never!" answered Ozma closing her lips firmly. "Never!" At this, Ruggedo, with a furious mutter touched his magic belt and where the Scarecrow had been there was nothing but a bale of hay.

"Will you speak now?" hissed the gnome. Ozma, instead of answering, merely shook her head again and this time Scraps vanished and in her place slumped a faded old rag bag. With a cry of dismay Peter saw the Cowardly Lion change into an iron dog and his good friend the

Iffin into a china cat. Then as the gnome stared vengefully up at him, his heart stood still. Good-bye to Oz and to Philadelphia. Good-bye to his grandfather, to Samuel Salt and Ato. Good-bye to all his fun and plans and his future as an air pilot. But before Ruggedo could open his mouth, the throne room doors burst violently apart.

"Drop that stick!" thundered a terrible voice, and the Gnome King was seized from behind and lifted bodily into the air. down clattered the conjurer's cane, and as the Oz folk, suddenly released from the enchantment, surged joyfully forward, the yellow bird inside Pigasus struck the quarter hour and loudly and defiantly screamed: "Cuckoo!"

CHAPTER 18
The Pirate Ship Arrives

A LL the time Peter and Pigasus had been flying toward the Emerald City, the *Crescent Moon*, as we happen to know, was not far behind. Without sinking, plunging to earth or misadventure of any kind it moved like a phantom ship through the azure skies of the loveliest Fairyland out of the world, reaching the Emerald City soon after Peter himself. But though Ato and Samuel feverishly furled sail and tugged at the wheel, though Roger screamed with vigor and vexation, the ship refused to stop

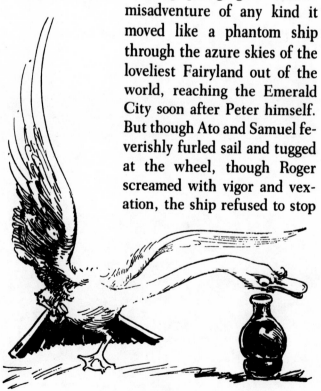

and sailed straight over the capital so that soon it was no more than a glittering dot in the distance.

"Great goozlebugs, Sammy, are we to fly on and on forever?" gulped Ato, mopping his hot forehead with his apron. "We're halfway over the Munchkin country now and if we keep this up we'll shoot straight out of this Imagi-Nation and land in some real country where no one will believe in us at all."

"Some real dangerous country," chattered the Read Bird, fluttering his feathers wildly. "Why don't you do something? Why don't you do something?" Samuel and Ato did not even bother to answer Roger's frenzied question, for they had all they could do to hold the wheel of the *Crescent Moon* steady. And after an exasperated glance at the two chiefs, Roger flew down to the pirate's cabin. "I'll just have a look at that flask," decided Roger bravely. The flask lay where it had fallen on the floor and picking it up Roger peered cautiously inside. The bottle seemed to be perfectly empty and locating the cork, Roger placed them side by side on Peter's berth and settled down beside them to think. Standing on one leg with his claw to his head, the Read Bird thought and thought so hard and intensely that his head feathers rose on end and waved to and fro. But just as the *Crescent Moon* reached the Deadly Desert on the other side of Oz, a perfectly splendid idea popped into his mind. Whirling out of

203

a porthole he flapped his wings to attract the attention of the pirate and Ato.

"Turn the ship around," screamed Roger imperiously. "We don't have to fly only in one direction. We can at least keep over the Land of Oz!" Ato and Samuel exchanged startled glances. Roger's advice was so sensible that they were surprised they had not thought of it themselves, and in a twinkling they had the *Crescent Moon* turned completely around and speeding in the opposite direction. With a little chuckle of satisfaction Roger returned to the cabin and to his thinking. "Now then," he reasoned solemnly, "we flew up because the cork came out of this bottle. Mouse ears and monkey whiskers! Huzza and Hurrah! I have it! If we flew up when the cork came out of the bottle why wouldn't we fly down if we put the cork back?" Dazzled by his own cleverness, Roger was about to make the experiment when another thought struck him, such a horrid thought that he almost gave up the idea entirely. Suppose they dropped so hard and suddenly that the *Crescent Moon* smashed to bits, and so far from the Emerald City that they would never reach the capital in time to do any good? "This is a ticklish matter," muttered Roger, opening and shutting his fan tail nervously, "but nevertheless I shall manage it." Taking the cork in one claw and the bottle in the other, he flew out on deck and setting both on a coil of rope squinted earnestly over the rail. "Good!" The *Crescent Moon* was again approaching the Emerald City. As they sailed majestically over the spacious gardens of the castle, Roger lifted the cork and slowly began to move it toward the top of the flask. Ato and the pirate, busy at the wheel, hardly noticed him, but gave little grunts and exclamations of astonishment as the great boat moved gradually downward. Nearer and nearer to the bottle came the cork. Nearer and nearer to the garden slanted the *Crescent Moon*, and when, with a tremulous gasp, Roger fitted the cork in the bottle, the ship settled grandly and gently in a waving bed of tulips.

"Well, shiver my liver!" beamed the pirate, while Ato, still holding the wheel, stared around in dazed disbelief and bewilderment.

"Not a shiver of any sort, if you ask me," exulted Roger briskly. "But hurry along. Let's move. The first thing to do is to find this Gnome King, and the next thing is to snatch his magic stick and belt. Don't stand staring at me like that! I brought the ship down to earth by putting the cork back in the bottle. Simple enough when you come to think of it."

"Simple enough! Why, the bird's a genius!" roared Ato, running over to press Roger's claw. "The Queen shall hear of this!"

"That she shall," cried Samuel Salt, giving the Read Bird such a clap between the wings that he was nearly thrown off the rail.

"Not unless you fellows hurry," twittered Roger, trying not to feel flattered. "She may be

enchanted or captured by this time. Come along!
Come along! Come along!" Realizing the neces-
sity for speed and action the three climbed over
the rail of the *Crescent Moon* and made a dash
for the Royal Castle of Oz and in less then a
minute were inside. From the throne room the
harsh voice of the Gnome King came echoing
out to them. Breaking into a run, Samuel Salt
reached the locked golden doors, put his great
shoulders against them and with one tremendous shove broke them open. And it was the
pirate who grasped Ruggedo and shook him so
violently that the conjurer's stick fell out of his
hand. Then Roger, wise old bird that he was,
unclasped the magic belt from the gnome's waist
and, flying straight for the ruler of Oz, dropped
it in her lap.

> "How did you get here so quick and so
> soon?
> Ho, everyone, look, here's the Man in the
> Moon,"

cried Peter, scarcely able to believe his own eyes.
"The *Crescent Moon*," corrected Samuel Salt,
smiling with relief to see his young shipmate
safe and hearty. "Come on down off that pig and
talk like yourself. Shiver my liver, I thought
you'd be a gollywog by this time."
"How, oh how, can we ever thank you?"
breathed Ozma, half rising from her throne,
while all the celebrities crowded around their
three rescuers. "I see you are pirates, too." The

"How can we ever thank you?" breathed Ozma

fairy looked in bewilderment from Ato to Samuel
Salt and cast a long serious look at Roger, now
contentedly perched on the King's shoulder.
"Then why—?"

"Then why did we help you, I suppose you
mean?" beamed Ato, snatching off his apron and
throwing it behind him. "Because we would not
have anyone on the throne of Oz but your sweet
and gracious self. That's why."

"*You* don't talk like a pirate," said Dorothy,
coming closer to Ato. "He's not!" cried Peter,
jumping off Pigasus, for he was dreadfully tired
of making verses. "Ato is King of the Octagon
Isle and the best cook this side of Philadelphia.
Girl! Girl! You should taste his pies and gin-
gerbread. And this is Captain Salt, a pirate, an
explorer, an ablebodied seamen and everything!"
Proudly Peter took an arm of each of his shipmates and with a little wave at Roger introduced
the Royal Reader of the Octagon Isle.

"But I still don't understand," sighed Ozma,
her eyes travelling slowly from Ato's bristling
beard to his rough pirate clothes.

"It's the whiskers," Peter assured her. With
a little chuckle he put his arm around the King.
"Just wait till he's taken off his beard and put
on his crown. "You'll see—"

"And what do I do with this?" boomed Samuel
Salt, holding out the squirming, kicking, muttering gnome.

"Let's change him into something quiet," suggested Peter, as Ruggedo's screams grew more

piercing. "Then we can decide what to do."

"I believe I will," mused Ozma, settling back on her throne. "Then we can talk in peace and hear all that our—our kind rescuers have to say." At Ozma's words Ruggedo gave a blood curdling screech, but no one felt sorry when Ozma touched her magic belt and the wicked gnome disappeared, leaving Samuel Salt holding by the handle a grey stone water jug.

"You should have turned him into a cuckoo clock," choked Pigasus, rolling over and over on the floor to relieve his feelings. With a little exclamation of sympathy Ozma touched her magic belt again, speaking a few low words. Whizz! whirr! Back to the fallen Clock Man sped the Yellow Bird, and had no sooner returned to its place before the Wise Man of Menankypoo jumped to his feet and fled like a gundersnatch from the throne room.

"Shall I catch him?" asked Peter as Pigasus, snorting his thanks and appreciation flew up on a green sofa and flapped his wings like a rooster.

"No, let him go," decided the fairy. "If we want him again I can summon him with the magic belt. Now I must disenchant the others." In four quick sentences, Ozma brought the Scarecrow, Scraps, the Cowardly Lion and the Iffin to themselves, and then, with everyone talking at once, the Oz folk tried to discover how Samuel and Ato and Roger and Peter and Pigasus had arrived so opportunely in the Emerald City; while the crew of the *Crescent Moon* tried to find out how Ruggedo had captured the capital and what had become of the pirates and Octagon Islanders.

"Has Your Majesty seen aught of eight fishermen, eight servitors, eight councillors, eight courtiers, eight shopkeepers, eight musicians, eight sailors, eight soldiers, eight scholars and poets and eight farmers?" called Ato above the terrible hub-bub and chatter.

"And fifty-eight pirates!" roared Samuel Salt, waving the jug that was Ruggedo wildly around his head.

> "Eighty and fifty-eight, fellows, you'll have
> to wait
> If we're to get this straight. One at a time!
> How did this pirate, King, bird, pig and
> Peter bring
> Help just in time?"

demanded the Patchwork Girl, turning a handspring and apparently no worse for her transformation.

"Yes, one at a time. That's the idea," agreed the Scarecrow, sidling up to Peter. "You tell what happened to you and then we'll tell what happened to us. How would that be?"

"How is it that girl can make verses when she's not riding me?" squealed Pigasus excitedly.

"It's the way she's made," whispered Dorothy, who had slipped down on the sofa beside the pink pig. "Sh-h, Ozma wants to say something." Ozma, upset and shocked as she had

SCRAPS TURNED A HANDSPRING

211

been by the unhappy events of the last hour, had now regained her composure.

"Let Peter and his friends tell their story," directed Ozma, raising her scepter for silence, "and let us all—" Ozma looked reprovingly at the Patchwork Girl, "let us all keep quite still until they do."

CHAPTER 19
Capital Times in the Capital

A LOUD cheer greeted the boy as he stepped forward, for Peter had saved the kingdom twice before and was not only a great favorite, but a great hero in the Emerald City of Oz. So  much had happened since he landed on Ato's Island that he scarcely knew where to begin. The celebrities, however, were so curious, so interested and so impatient to hear all about everything that he simply cleared his throat and plunged right into the story, telling all that had occurred on the strange islands which the *Crescent*

Moon had passed and visited. The Oz folk cast sympathetic and approving glances at the handsome pirate and the jolly old King as Peter explained how they had both been robbed and deserted, and all listened spellbound to his spirited and detailed account of the cruise on the pirate ship. The Wizard of Oz shook his head thoughtfully over Shell City and the bananny goat. Ozma was deeply interested in the castle boat of the Duke of Dork, while Dorothy and Trot could hardly wait to ride Pigasus and hear themselves talking in verse. Of Menankypoo, Peter could tell them very little, and after relating what Binx and Peggo had told, he turned eagerly to Samuel Salt.

"I left you and Ato and Roger in Menankypoo. Now, how in Oz did you ever get here?" demanded the boy, who had been trying to puzzle this mystery out for himself all the time he was telling his story.

"On the *Crescent Moon*," answered the pirate, grinning down at his mate and cabin boy. "How else would an able-bodied seaman travel? Ha!"

"But without any water?" questioned Peter incredulously.

"Aye, aye, mate! Without any water," rasped Roger, touching his forehead with his claw. "We flew through the sky! Aye! Aye! Sky high!"

"It was that cask you brought ashore," explained Samuel Salt, seeing that the curiosity of Peter and the whole company was growing well nigh unbearable. "That flask and Roger's cleverness brought us here. Why, shiver my liver, had it not been for that bird we'd have been flying yet and forever!" If the celebrities had been thrilled by Peter's story they were even more excited when the pirate described the flight of the *Crescent Moon* through the skyways of Oz and the masterly manner in which Roger had solved the problem of landing in time and in safety. And when Samuel concluded, Roger was given such a round of applause that he grew positively embarrassed and put his head under his wing. Ato came in for his share of cheering, too, and feeling well repaid for all their trials and vicissitudes, the four shipmates sat down on the sofa beside Dorothy and Pigasus while the Scarecrow told the other side of the story.

The Gnome King's army had taken the capital by surprise and before word of his arrival had even reached the castle, the Octagon Islanders and pirates had overpowered Ozma's gentle citizens and locked them up in their houses and shops. Then, hidden from view by some of the conjurer's magic, Ruggedo and the Clock Man had entered the castle unseen and stolen the magic belt. Ozma and her councillors were in the throne room at the time, choosing a ruler for a new kingdom in the Gillikin Country and the first knowledge they had of the Gnome King's presence was when he and the Wise Man of Menankypoo burst into the conference. Brandishing his dagger and tapping his magic belt the gnome had threatened them with instant

transformation and destruction, and no sooner
had the Scarecrow and Tin Woodman attempted
to seize the little villain than the Cuckoo Clock
Man had raised the conjurer's stick and brought
them all to a standstill. The only thing that had
saved the Oz folk had been Ruggedo's boastful-
ness. The gnome had not been able to resist this
opportunity of telling his old enemies how he
had at last outwitted them and taken their city,
and what he intended to do once he was Ruler
and Emperor of Oz.

"And that is what he was doing when Peter
came flying in on the pig," finished the Scarecrow, pushing back his old straw hat.

"And right after that he turned you to a bale
of hay," Peter reminded him seriously.

"Yes," sighed the Scarecrow, ruefully rubbing his knees. "I can still feel those cords, but
that about clears up everything, does it not, my
dear?" Ozma smiled as the Scarecrow thus in-
formally addressed her.

"Well, I don't quite understand how Ruggedo
recovered his speech," mused the little Princess
of Oz thoughtfully, "nor how he crossed the
desert—"

"Or what he did to the pirates and Octagon
Islanders," added Peter, staring hard at the stone
jug which, strangely enough, had Ruggedo's face
on the spout. "I only saw two when I flew over
the city."

"Yes, what has he done with our men?"
wheezed Ato, jumping up so suddenly that the

Read Bird tumbled from his shoulder into Dorothy's lap.

"Fetch in those pirates," commanded Ozma sternly, at which the Soldier with Green Whiskers, stepping out from behind the throne where he had been hiding all afternoon, started reluctantly for the garden. Peter, knowing the grand army of old, and realizing how exceedingly timid and nervous he was, ran quickly to help him and presently they returned with the two pirates, very ragged and downcast, between them. At sight of their old captain the buccaneers trembled violently and tried to pull away, but a word from the ruler of Oz made them straighten up and in faltering voices describe the capture of the city. Without rest or stop, Ruggedo had marched his army from Menankypoo to the capital. The Deadly Desert had been crossed on a way-word which Ruggedo had learned from the Cuckoo Clock Man. With uneasy glances at Ozma and Samuel Salt, they explained how they had driven the Ozites into their dwellings and how Ruggedo, instead of rewarding the pirates and Octagon Islanders, had turned them all into cobblestones—all, that is, except the two who had guarded the gates. Those two were to receive a bag of emeralds apiece for their trouble.

"And where are these cobblestones?" inquired Ozma sternly.

"Just inside Your Majesty's garden," mumbled the first pirate glumly.

"A hard fate, but good enough for them,"

217

ticked the Copper Man, in his mechanical way. "Let us build a mon-u-ment of these cob-ble stones to warn all peo-ple not to re-bel against their ru-lers."

"Oh, I hope Your Highness will not do that!" puffed Ato anxiously. "I am sure they are sorry now, and will not trouble you again."

The two pirates, much to Peter's amusement nodded vigorously, so Ozma, by means of her magic belt, transformed the Gnome King's army to their proper forms and Peter and the Scarecrow ran off to lead them to the throne room. A more ragged, dusty, discouraged band of rebels it would have been hard to discover. The Octagon Islanders failed to recognize in the burly pirate beside Peter their former kindly monarch. But when Ato made himself known to them, Sixentwo fell upon his knees and humbly begged for pardon and forgiveness on behalf of the subjects.

"All we desire," sniffed the tattered and tired old councillor, "is to return to to our island and our homes. We've had enough of conquering and ambition. And if Your Majesty will take us back we will promise to serve and obey you for the rest of our unnatural lives."

"There, there!" murmured Ato, pulling Sixentwo to his feet and feeling terribly sorry for his poor, disillusioned subjects. "Say no more about it, old fellow. But you'll have to do without me for six months of the year, for I've taken a notion to go exploring, and if Sammy will have me I intend to spend half of my time as cook on the *Crescent Moon*."

"Why, goosewing my tops'ls! That's the best news I've heard since I landed in Oz!" roared the pirate, clasping Ato affectionately round his great middle.

"No, it's not! No, it's not!" Jumping to her feet Ozma raised her scepter. "I have some better news! I hereby decree that Samuel Salt shall give up piracy and become our Royal Discoverer and Explorer, take possession of new countries and set the flag of Oz on far islands and mountain tops."

" 'Ray! 'Ray! Hurray!" shouted the company, stamping their feet and throwing up their hats and handkerchiefs. "Three cheers for Samuel Salt, Royal Explorer and Discoverer for Oz!"

"Oh, he'll like that!" exulted Peter, rushing over to shake Samuel's hand, and if the pirates

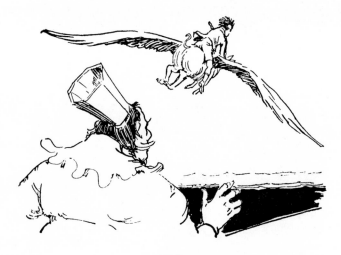

looked a little sulky and disconsolate nobody took any notice of them. Indeed, as both they and the Octagon Islanders were too downcast and unhappy to enjoy so gay and carefree a crowd, Ozma transported the first to their island homes— not forgetting the women and children locked up in the conjurer's cave—and the second back to the *Sea Lion* in the harbor of Menankypoo. Then, because she felt so relieved and happy over the way everything was turning out, the Princess ordered a grand feast in honor of Peter and Pigasus, Ato, Roger and Samuel Salt, Royal Explorer of Oz.

CHAPTER 20
Farewell to Oz

PETER had a chance to renew at the party his friendships with many of his old chums and comrades. The Iffin was so delighted to see the boy from Philadelphia that he shed tears of joy into the soup, while Jack Pumpkinhead lit the candle inside his pumpkin to remind Peter of the exciting adventures they had had together in Chimneyville and Baffleburg. Ato, who loved both feasting and stories, had his fill of both and spent the most interesting and enjoyable evening of his life listening to the stories of the celebrites, the Princesses and famous beasts of Oz. Ruggedo, now a handsome stone jug, was passed curiously from hand to hand and then, at the Scarecrow's suggestion, filled with delicious Ozade. And I am quite sure it was the first time the Gnome King was filled with anything so good, sweet and sparkling. Trot, mounted on Pigasus, flew around and round the table making such merry rhymes that Scraps had all she could do to answer them. And not till everyone was rested and refreshed did Ozma return to the more serious business of repairing all the damage done by the mischievous little gnome. Summoning Clocker with the magic belt Ozma forced him to reveal how Ruggedo had recovered his speech, and after he had struck several times she turned him over to the Wizard, who promised to replace his bad works with good ones, and so he probably will become a useful and interesting addition to the castle. You can see yourself how useful a walking clock would be on picnics and trips.

"He'll make a twin for you, Tik Tok," chuckled the Wizard, as he dragged Clocker determinedly off to his laboratory. The standing stick and the magic cask that had brought the *Crescent Moon* to Oz were carefully placed in the emerald safe and the Hardy-hood, which had protected Ruggedo from everything but magic, was presented to Roger as a slight token of appreciation for all he had done to save the Emerald City.

Next, the Menankypoos were brought up out

of the sea and their treasure restored to them. Samual Salt promised on his way back to stop and see that the rightful King was placed on the throne. But Ozma felt sure the inhabitants of the strange little country would be glad enough to have their old sovereign back. In the morning she promised to sent the *Crescent Moon* to the Nonestic Ocean so that Samuel could start on his first voyage of discovery. Then Samuel, who felt a little uneasy about his men, expressed a desire to see the pirates and running upstairs they all looked curiously in the magic picture while Ozma commanded it to reveal the buccaneers. It showed the pirates, bad to the end, sailing away under full sail in the *Sea Lion*.

"Ah, well," rumbled Samuel Salt regretfully. "Let them go. Pirating is all they know or care about. I'll pick me a crew of able-bodied seamen right in this town. I've a cook and a lookout already," he finished, with a wink at Ato and the Read Bird. But Ozma had other ideas and without saying a word of her intentions, changed the pirates into sea gulls.

"Now they can still have the sea that they love and yet do no harm to other ships and kingdoms," decided the Princess wisely. It was long past midnight by now, and even Ato, fond as he was of story telling, began to yawn and grow drowsy. As the merry company began to break up and wish one another good-night, Peter slipped up to Ozma. He felt that he could not say good-bye to his old shipmates—that rather than say good-bye to Samuel, Ato, Roger and Pigasus, he would go before they missed him.

"I hate to leave," sighed Peter, with a regretful look down the long, gay table. "But my grandfather must be worried about me and the team needs me, too. So, if you don't mind, I'll just dust along—and thanks a lot for everything. You'll be good to Pigasus, won't you? And some time, when Samuel is going on a real long voyage, wish me to Oz again!"

"I promise!" Solemnly Ozma nodded and smiled. "Next time bring your grandfather with you," whispered the fairy, surely the most understanding and discerning little lady in Oz. "You might even teach us to play baseball," she added mischievously, "and then you could stay here with us always."

"Maybe I could," mused Peter slowly with a long look at Samuel Salt and Ato. "Maybe next

time I will stay!" Then, as he felt himself beginning to vanish, he raised one arm and with
a long "Cheerio!" dropped out of sight and Oz
into his own four post bed in Philadelphia. And
that is all I know of the story. But imagine! the
pearls he found in Shell City were real pearls,
and the thoughtful ruler of Oz transported them
with him. My, I should like to have been there
when he woke up and found them!

THE INTERNATIONAL WIZARD OF OZ CLUB

The International Wizard of Oz Club was founded in 1957 to bring together all those interested in Oz, its authors and illustrators, film and stage adaptations, toys and games, and associated memorabilia. From a charter group of 16, the club has grown until today it has over 2200 members of all ages throughout the world. Its magazine, *The Baum Bugle*, first appeared in June 1957 and has been published continuously ever since. The *Bugle* appears three times a year and specializes in popular and scholarly articles about Oz and its creators, biographical and critical studies, first edition checklists, research into the people and places within the Oz books, etc. The magazine is illustrated with rare photographs and drawings, and the covers are in full color. The Oz Club also publishes a number of other Oz-associated items, including full-color maps; an annual collection of original Oz stories; books; and essays.

Each year, the Oz Club sponsors conventions in different areas of the United States. These gatherings feature displays of rare Oz and Baum material, an Oz quiz, showings of Oz films, an auction of hard-to-find Baum and Oz items, much conversation about Oz in all its aspects, and many other activities.

The International Wizard of Oz Club appeals to the serious student and collector of Oz as well as to any reader interested in America's own fairyland. For further information, please send a *long* self-addressed stamped envelope to:

Fred M. Meyer, Executive Secretary
THE INTERNATIONAL WIZARD
   OF OZ CLUB
Box 95
Kinderhook, IL 62345